OTHER BOOKS BY T

Native American

Across The River
Apache Pride
Beyond The Heart
Within The Heart (Sequel to Beyond the Heart)
Broken Feather
Cherokee Courage
Dream Catcher Woman
Emboldened Heart
Gentle Savage
Son of Silver Fox (sequel to Gentle Savage)
Gedi Puniku (Cat Eyes)
Impossible Promise
Kiowa White Moon
Kiowa Wind Walker
Little Flower
No Price Too High
Paiute Passion
Papago Promise
Plenty Proud
Sagebrush Serenade
Savage Land
Shadow Hawk
Shoshone Surrender
Spirit Dancer
White Hawk and the Star Maiden

Historical or Regency/Victorian Romance Books

A Bride for Windridge Hall
Defiant Heart
Highroad
Indentured
The Deception
The Fledgling
Wild Irish Rose
Winslow's Web

Contemporary Western Romance Books

Georgie Girl
Grasping at Straws
Mattie
Passion's Pride
Single-handed Heart

Historical Western Romance Books

Elusive Innocents

20th Century Historical Romance Books

Italy Vacation
Moments of Misconception
Radcliff Hall
Reluctant Flapper
Samuel's Mansion
Taxi Dancer

Action and Adventure Mystery Romance Books

Ghost Island
Holding On
Payback

THE LOCKED ROOM

Jeanie P.Johnson

Jeanie P. Johnson

Futuristic Action and Adventure Romance Books

Chosen
Pony Up
Project Rat Pack
Surviving
The Division
The Dominion
The Mechanism

Time travel/Reincarnation Romance Books

Egyptian Key
Letters From The Grave
Seekers
Seekers Two
Seekers Three
The Vortex-book One

Non Fiction Books

A Collection of short stories (some true)
Chief Washakie (short history of Shoshoni Chief)
Dream Symbols Made Easy (how to analyze dreams)
Peaches (inspirational)
The Prune Pickers (my childhood)
Whimper (true story of racial conflicts)

Children's Picture Book

Dandy The Horse
Monster In My Closet
The Hen Mrs. Cackle

Jeanie P. Johnson

Story by

Jeanie P. Johnson

Jeanie P. Johnson

CHAPTER ONE

La Jolla California
1980

Loraine looked at the small piece of paper in her hand, with the address scribbled on it. It wasn't that far from La Jolla Shores and she thought how exciting it would be to actually live in the magnificent house that stood before her, overlooking the beach and ocean. There was something welcoming about it, and even a little familiar. She crossed her fingers, as she got out of her little VW bug, and walked up the steps that lead to the front porch, hoping that she would be hired by the woman who put the advertisement into the newspaper. She counted the steps as she climbed. Twenty steps, the same as her age, she thought absently. The house looked old, at least a hundred years old, she figured, and it looked pretty rundown from her vantage point, but it was so blocked from view by Bougainville, rambling roses, tall ornamental grasses, and ivy twisting about the porch columns, that she could barely see the actual walls of the house. A variety of ice plants, and other succulent greenery, all in bloom with a mad variety of colors, cascaded down the rock garden that lined the long entrance steps which she was climbing. The house itself was a two story, with an upper floor above that, probably an attic, Loraine thought.

The first floor, rambled out in both directions, from the entry, blocked by trees that shaded it, which seemed to be in competition with the overgrowth of all the other plants around the house. The second story was a beautiful combination of windows, looking out against the beach. She knew the view would be breathtaking, and couldn't wait to experience it. The center window was a large bay window, and the others were smaller with leaded pains, made in a diamond pattern, typical of the era it was built in. It had two tall chimneys one at either end of the house, and it was built of brick and stone, which seemed to have been taken from native stone of the area, when the house was built, since much of it matched the stones she saw in the rock garden. A retaining wall, made of the same stone, held the front yard from slipping down the embankment that led down to the road, and much of the succulent plants from the rock garden cascaded down over the edge of the wall, almost hiding it with the years of growth that had not been regulated by a gardener's hand.

Loraine reached the large entrance door, and paused before she rang the bell. She made sure her skirt was straight, and that her white blouse was tucked neatly under the belt of her skirt. She glanced down at her low heels, hitched her purse up onto her shoulder, patted her sandy blond hair to make sure it was in place, and took a deep breath, then pushed the button. She could hear the chimes of a musical sounding door bell, which made her shiver in its familiarity, but then most door bells sounded similar, she chided. The ringing echoed in her ears, and then she heard footsteps approaching the door. Through the chiseled and sandblasted rose design of the side windows, that encased the door frame, she could see the distorted figure of someone approaching the door. When it opened, an elderly woman stood before Loraine.

"Amelia Landon?" Loraine questioned.

"No, I am the housekeeper, Mary Mathews," she explained. "Come this way, Miss Landon is expecting you."

Loraine followed the housekeeper through the entrance hall, as the sound of their footsteps reverberated against the smooth marble tiles, and she tried to take in all that surrounded her, while she walked into the room Mary Mathews indicated, right off the entrance hall. The room was not very bright, because the windows were so shaded by all the plants and trees that grew up around them, and Loraine had to adjust her eyes to the dimness of the room, after coming out of the bright sunlight of the California beach town.

Mary left her, and she stood looking around the room. It was as though she had been transported back in time when she saw the old furniture that dated back to the 20's and beyond that, she thought. The piano, an old upright, which drew her eyes first, stood in the corner and had a fringed shawl with a busy design of a combination of bright colors, thrown across the top, draping down over the front, with a large collection of photographs in a fascinating array of different size and shaped frames scattered over the cloth. Amid the frames were a couple of vases with no flowers in them and a few figurines of an older era, hiding here and there. The couch also had a bright fringed shawl draped over the back, covering the deep rose-colored velvet upholstery with raised flowers in the pattern. Satin throw pillows with fringe around the edges and pictures painted on them, which were popular souvenirs back in the twenty's and thirty's, were placed haphazardly on the couch. The two side chairs also had raised patterns but they were a deep green. The room, which was rather large, seemed smaller, because it was so full of different sizes of odd shaped tables with a menagerie of porcelain animals, small vases, figurines, glob music boxes, that she was sure, if turned upside down showered down flakes of some sort onto the miniature scene inside the globs, placed in no particular order on their surfaces. Small book cases were up against the wall, at least three of them, also filled with books, and other collections of the same things that littered the tables. The mantle over a large fireplace, which dominated the room, was filled with antique china dolls, more picture frames, a small carved wooden carousel horse, an ornate tea pot along with cup and saucer to match, faded Birthday cards from many years gone by, a wooden solider, holding a drum, and a small stuffed teddy bear. Nothing in the room seemed to follow any particular design or theme, but appeared as though someone opened a trunk of old odds and ends, and proceeded to place them about the room.

But what was most unusual, was a low table pushed up against the far wall, and on it was a rather large doll house that looked exactly like the house she had just entered. Upon closer inspection, Loraine saw that the very room she stood in was miniaturized in the doll house, with the same kind of furniture the room held. The only difference was that there was not the large collection of things sitting on all the surfaces in the doll house, but there were a few things, like miniature pictures on the piano, under which the same colored shawl was spread, and a few miniature figurines placed on the tables, and little wooden books in the book cases. Even the pictures hanging on the wall of the doll house were the same ones, sized down, that were on the walls of the unusual room. The only thing that wasn't in the identical room of the doll house was another doll house. There was nothing in the replica, where the doll house stood.

Loraine was fascinated by the doll house and stooped, looking into each room, as though taking a tour of the house itself. There was only one room in the doll house that had nothing in it, while all the other rooms were full of furnishings and pictures, and all other sorts of things that decorated the little home, which Loraine was sure, matched the house itself, just as the things in this room matched the ones in the doll house.

"I see you have found my prize possession," Loraine heard a voice behind her say.

She had not heard anyone come into the room, and she swung around to discover, a woman, in her late seventies or early eighties, sitting in a wheelchair, with a throw blanket on her knees, staring up at her. In spite of her age, she seemed spry, as she wheeled herself up to where Loraine was standing.

"Do you like my doll house?" she asked with a friendly smile on her face, which seemed to bring youth to her features, as the soft aged skin stretched across her delicate bone structure.

The woman's white hair was pulled back in a lose bun at the nap of her neck, and Loraine was surprised at the thickness of the tresses. She wore a light blue dress, which reflected the style of the thirty's, with lace across the V neckline, padded shoulders, and an old fashion broach pinned at the point of the V. The color matched her pale blue eyes that looked bright, and showed no sign of age, but sparkled, as though she found amusement in what she was looking at.

"I have never seen anything like it, except maybe at Knots Berry Farm," Loraine said truthfully, as she gave the woman a pleased smile.

"And you won't either, because I have designed it myself. I mean all the things inside of the doll house. My grandfather built the house for me when I was young. But I have spent a life time filling it with everything to match the house I live in. Because of that, nothing should ever be changed in this house, or I would have to make new furnishings to match, you understand. I will explain about it later. For now, come here, so I can look at you."

Loraine obeyed, and stepped forward into a shaft of light that filtered through the one small part of the side window where it was not covered with some sort of plant or tree. Amelia Landon gave her an appraising look, as she nodded approvingly. She was intrigued to discover, that this young girl seemed to look a little like she did, when she was young, before she was committed to the wheelchair she was a prisoner of.

"You say that your name is Loraine Miller?"

Amelia took a pair of glasses out of her pocket, and put them on her nose as she took a closer look at Loraine, admiring her thick sandy colored hair, which even though it was held back by a ribbon behind her head, still cascaded down in waves past her waist in back. She noted the light scattering of freckles over the small pert nose, and the vivid green eyes, that looked innocent yet knowing, at the same time. She was dressed neatly and seemed to be confident, the kind of person Amelia liked.

"Yes."

"Well, that settles it then. I will just have to hire you!"

"You are not going to interview me?" Loraine was taken aback at the woman's sudden decision.

"Of course not, the moment I heard your name, I knew I would hire you. Don't look so surprised. My mother's name was Loraine, and it is about my mother that has prompted me to look for a companion in the first place."

Loraine wondered if the old woman was a little senile. "I...I don't quite understand," she stammered.

"Of course you don't! How do you expect to understand it until I explain it all to you?" She laughed softly, and rolled her wheelchair over to the door, and closed it. "Don't want Mary listening to anything, the old biddy. You would think she was my jailor, not my housekeeper!" She turned her wheelchair to face Loraine. "Go ahead and sit down, there on the couch," she encouraged, as she wheeled up to the couch herself.

Loraine sat down, staring into the eyes of the woman as they twinkled at her. The old woman winked, throwing Loraine off guard.

"Well now. I saw you were looking at the doll house. What did you see that was unusual about it?"

Loraine shrugged. "Everything! I could see that everything in this room matched the room in the doll house, so I assume that all the other rooms match as well."

"Except for one room..." Loraine pointed a bony finger at the empty room. "There is one room that has nothing in it. Do you know why? Of course you don't."

"Because that room in the house is empty as well?" Loraine guessed.

"No, because I have never been in that room of the house."

Loraine raised her eyebrows. "Really? I assume you have lived here a very long time though..."

"Since the day I was born, but I have never been in that room, so of course I can't put anything in the doll house room, until I find out what is in there!"

"But why, it's your house isn't it? You could go in any room you want!"

"You would think so, but I have been in this wheelchair since I was sixteen years old, and since that day, I have never been upstairs, and therefore could never go in that room. Before I was sixteen, I was forbidden to go in that room. It was my mother's room, you know."

"No...I didn't know."

"Well, it was her room. And her name was Loraine, just like yours. Loraine Marie Landon. I never met my mother. She died when I was born."

"Oh, I am sorry."

"I am sorry too, because I know nothing about her. My

grandparents would not tell me anything about her, except for calling her horrible names and claiming I was a bastard. Don't look so shocked. I am…and that is what frustrates me. My father was not a Landon. My mother was. I don't know who my father is, and I know nothing about my mother, except that she lived in this house and that she had a room in this house, which was locked on the day she died. All her pictures were taken down, and locked in that room. My grandparents erased her from their memory and never allowed me to have a memory of her. That is how I ended up in this chair. I was trying to find out about her. Trying to pick the lock on her door, and just as I managed to get it to open, my grandfather discovered me, pushed me aside with such force, as he eagerly relocked the door, that I lost my balance and fell down the stairs, breaking my back, and have been in this wheelchair ever since.

"Up until that moment, I loved exploring the house, but my mother's room was the only room I had never gotten to see. My grandfather felt remorse about accidentally knocking me down the stairs, so he built the doll house for me. He took pictures of all the rooms, so I could remember what they looked like, except for my mother's room, and he gave me the material to furnish the doll house just like the house, as something to keep me occupied, since I couldn't walk. As for my mother's room, it remained locked, and the key was hidden away, or thrown away, I don't know which, and since I could never make it upstairs anyway, there was no way that I could discover what the room looked like. Even if I could, Mary, my jailor, would never allow me access to it. She promised my grandfather on his death bed that she would not allow me in the room for as long as she was here, and since she is younger than I am, she will outlive me, and I shall never get to look upon my mother's room, or learn anything about her."

"That is horrible! Why don't you just fire the house keeper and hire another one?" Loraine asked feeling astounded that someone from the grave could still control this poor woman.

"Because it was in the will. Mary was promised she could remain here until the day she died, if she chose to, and she chose to. So there you have it."

"So what does that all have to do with hiring me?" Loraine wanted to know.

"It occurred to me, that I would die and never lay eyes on that room. I would die knowing nothing about my mother, or even what she looked like, because my grandfather hated her for some unknown reason. Mary certainly would never help me. She didn't even know my mother, being younger than me. She was hired a lot later, after I got older, but was always faithful to my grandfather. So I decided I would hire an accomplice, to help me get into that room and discover the truth about my past. Not only to discover the past, but I also want to finish the doll house, before

I die, and I can't do that room until I know what it looks like inside. Who better to hire than someone with my own mother's name? Of course I did not know that anyone with my mother's name would apply for the job as my companion, but the moment you told me your name on the phone, I knew you were the one I should hire. It was fate! You do believe in fate, don't you?"

"Not really, but if you believe in it...."

"Of course I believe in it! It is what has brought me to this sad situation in the first place! I have been a lonely old woman in a wheelchair, with no friends, and nothing to do with my time but work on that doll house, and collect things. Mary takes me out and sometimes Jasper, the handyman, will take me out too. To tell you the truth, he is not very handy. Just look how run down the place is! Well, never mind. When I die, this place will probably die with me. When I go out, I make the rounds of all the estate sales in the area, to collect things to decorate my home with, but as you can see, I am starting to run out of room to put them all."

"Why don't you have any friends?" Loraine thought it strange that she had lived here all her life and didn't know anyone enough to befriend them.

"I told you. I am a bastard, and my grandfather was ashamed of me. My grandmother was a mouse of a woman who allowed my grandfather to run things as he pleased. He would never allow me out of the house or anyone in to visit me. He had a tutor come in to teach me, and once I learned the rudiments of reading and math, I was left to my own devices to teach myself through all the books in the Library here. The only people I knew were the servants. None of those remain, and we only have a maid that comes in twice a week, and a cook that comes in to make dinner. Other than that, there is just me and Mary, and Jasper, who lives in a little house out back, where his shop is. I had never set foot out of this house, until after my grandfather died, and by that time, my grandmother was too feeble to protest. That was when I started buying things to bring back to the house. They were like the friends I never had. It is very hard to make friends when you are bound to a wheelchair. People pity you, or don't know what to say to you if they don't pity you. So now you will be my new found friend, Loraine, and your main purpose here is to help me find a way into that room, without Mary discovering it. She is such a bear, I don't dare cross her, or she will make my existence miserable."

Loraine was shocked, that this woman had no control of her own household, and must bow to the housekeeper, and couldn't even discover anything about her own mother! The challenge was exciting, and her heart went out to the woman in the wheelchair, because she would have hated being in her position.

Of course, she was no better off than Amelia, because her own mother had died when she was very young, but at least she had pictures of her, and knew who she was and everything that her father was able to tell her about her mother, before he died in an auto accident when she herself was sixteen. This made her feel a certain kindred feeling towards the old woman.

"Well, what do you say, Loraine? Are you game? Do you wish to help an old crippled woman break into a room in her own house?" She looked up expectantly at Loraine.

Loraine already knew what her answer would be. She had wanted to live in that house the moment she had seen it. It wasn't the first time she had seen the house. She had noticed it over the years, and always wondered who lived there, and what it looked like on the inside? She had never dreamed that one day she would actually get to meet the owner, and get to live there as well.

"I think this is going to be an exciting job," she confided. "And I will do everything in my power to learn about your mother. I was told that your grandfather used to be a very prominent man in these parts. He owned a shoe factory, I believe…"

"Yes, but not after I was born. By that time, the factory had gone under. It had caught on fire, and he never could get it back up and running again. He had to rely on his investments to stay afloat. At first it was difficult, the depression nearly did him in, but then, after the war, he invested in a little known company called IBM, and things took a turn for the better. Now it has all been left to me, and I have invested in Microsoft, a new upcoming development that is going to surpass IBM, I believe. It's based in Seattle. Not many people can afford a computer in their home, and less people know how to work one, but that was how television started out. No one had one, and now everyone has one in their home, and sometimes even more than one. You have to keep up with the times, you know, and try to look into the future."

Loraine found this woman an enigma, seeing as how she lived in a house that transported one back in time, and wore clothes out of the depression years, and with all the money she apparently had, her house was run down, and the garden wasn't even taken care of.

"If your grandfather was well known back in his day, I am sure there must have been things written about him in the newspaper. If I can find out something about him, I might be able to find out something about your mother as well. Affluent people often made the society page, because they set the trend."

"I was thinking that maybe my mother had a diary. If you could get into her room, you could look for one."

"Yes, but if there is no key…"

"Old houses like this one often had skeleton keys that would open most of the doors. I could never get to Mary's keys, but I am sure you could try your hand at it."

"I suppose that is a plan. When would you like me to move in?"

"As soon as you can, I am not getting any younger, you know."

"How old are you?" Loraine had been wondering her age from the moment the woman wheeled into the room.

"I will be eighty in three-months-time," Amelia admitted. "Sounds ancient, doesn't it?"

"My father always said that age was a frame of mind," Loraine smiled.

"Your father was a wise man," Amelia complemented. "I often still feel like I am sixteen on the inside, but my aching body, brings me up short sometimes, and I have to admit I am a lot older, after all!" She chuckled. "I envy youth, because I never really had a typical childhood, or was able to be a normal teenager. I never married, or had children, or even lived, in the real sense of the word, so I have no choice but to live through others, and I think I am going to enjoy living through you, young lady. You will breathe life into these old bones."

Loraine smiled kindly down at Amelia. "I will try to lighten your life, and if it is the last thing I do, I will discover everything about your mother that I can, before you die. Hopefully you will live to be a hundred!"

"Hopefully," Amelia agreed.

CHAPTER TWO

"Aunt Mel!" Loraine called as she tugged at the back kitchen door. "I got..." the sentence was not finished as she bumped into a complete stranger, in her aunt's kitchen. "Who...who are you?" she asked as he steadied her with one strong hand.

"Hi, Sweetie," her aunt smiled, right behind the stranger that had practically knocked Loraine over. "This is Larry...he's..."

"Lawrence, really, but your aunt insists on calling me Larry, for some unknown reason..." He put out his hand.

"Lawrence sounds so stuffy, don't you agree Sweetie? I hope you got the job, because I have just rented your old room to Larry here."

Loraine blinked. "What? What if I didn't get the job?" She questioned, feeling a little put out that her aunt had rented her room out, and she had not even moved out yet. She still had things in her room, for Christ sakes!

"Oh, you will get one eventually. You know we talked about it, you finding a live in job so I could rent out your room."

"But good grief, Aunt Mel, you could have at least waited

until I got the job!" Loraine insisted as she gave a side glance at Larry, or Lawrence, or whatever his name was.

"Oh yeah, this is Loraine, my niece, I was telling you about," Melanie mentioned to Lawrence, realizing she had not introduced Loraine to him even though she had told Loraine his name.

"So, you're just moving into my room, whether I have vacated it or not, huh?" she eyed him sarcastically, and rolled her eyes. "You and my aunt should get along just great!"

"Hey, I don't want to push you out or anything. I could find another room."

"Oh, no you don't" Melanie snapped. "You already agreed to take the room and paid me in advance. I'm not giving you your money back!"

"Aunt Mel!" Loraine fumed.

"What's going on here?" Randy had sauntered into the room, hearing the commotion from the living room, where he had been watching TV.

"Hey honey, meet Larry, he is going to be living in your cousin's room, as soon as she finds a job, so she can move out. Oh…if you didn't get hired, you can sleep in the den until you do. I told Larry he could move in right away."

Lawrence looked at Melanie, then Randy, and lastly at Loraine, and was starting to feel he had transplanted himself right in the middle of a family dispute, that he didn't want to be any part of. "I...I don't have to move in right away. I could stay at the motel until the room is vacant," he offered.

"No you can't. You have already paid me!" Melanie insisted.

"It doesn't matter," Loraine said at last, now that she could finally get a word in. "I got the job, so you, Larry, or Lawrence, or whoever you are, is welcome to my room. I just have to get the rest of my things, that I don't plan to take with me, and shove them in the basement, and then my wonderful room is all yours! You will probably want to redecorate it. You know, it being so girly and all. I'm sure pink is not your color."

Lawrence grinned at her, and she suddenly noticed how good looking he was, and how his dark eyes sparkled at her in amusement.

"Oh, I don't know, I sort of like pink," he teased.

"Good, then you will like my room just fine."

"I'm sure I will. Do you need help with getting the rest of your things out?"

"Oh aren't you champing at the bit? Can't wait to occupy my space huh?"

"No, I just wanted to be of some help, since it seems I am usurping your ..."

"Oh, don't bother yourself, Randy can help me, can't you

Randy?" Loraine gave Randy a look that said that if he said otherwise, he would have her to deal with.

"Oh…sure, sure, I am always at your service," he gave an exaggerated bow.

She grabbed his collar, and pulled him after her, as Lawrence watched with amused eyes. Too bad she was moving out, he thought. He would have liked to get to know her, but of course, there was always the chance that she would come and visit. He wondered if her relationship with her aunt was a strong one. The woman didn't seem to mind pushing her niece out, so she could rent the room to him. He hoped there was no bad blood between them, and that was why Loraine had decided to move out of her aunt's home.

"Don't pay any attention to her," Melanie laughed. "She's not mad. We love each other fine. It is just that since her uncle died, I have been having a hard time holding things together, and to tell you the truth, she needs to get out on her own and take life by the horns. I think the change will do her good. When her father died, that would be my late husband's brother, we happily took her in, but she is a big girl now. She has had a hard time knowing just what to do with her life, and hasn't held down any work for a very long period of a time, since she just can't find her niche, if you know what I mean. Anyway, I thought if she could find a job where she lived with someone, it would give her time to discover just what she wants to do with the rest of her life, without having to feel like she is dependent on me or anyone else, for that matter. She has pride, and I could tell it was all getting to her."

"Well, now I understand a little better. I hope she doesn't hate me for stealing her room."

"It was the only way to make sure she took that step," Melanie informed him. She liked Larry, and thought she could see a look of attraction in his eye for her niece. But Loraine didn't need a man just yet. She needed to find her own self. She had seemed so lost since her father died, and four years down the road, she still seemed lost. She needed to get out of her rut and start living again. She was starting to depend too much on Randy as her closest friend, and that worried Melanie.

"I didn't realize how anxious your mother was to get me out of the house," Loraine fumed at Randy, as he followed her up to her room.

"Come on, Rainy, she didn't mind you being here. We all love you. It is just time for you to spread your wings, is all. All little fledglings must hop out of the nest sometime, and you are a little overdue."

"You are one to talk! You are older than I am and still living at home!"

"You know I moved back when dad died to help mom out! That was uncalled for!"

"Ok, I am sorry, but to rent out my room before she even found out if I had gotten hired or not! That is a little pushy!"

"You know mom. Once she gets an idea in her head, she has to follow through before she gets sidetracked. I am sure she just wanted to gather up all the loose ends as soon as she could."

"There were no loose ends yet! She just wanted to unravel the whole sweater, so I would fall out!"

"Oh, I am sure there are reasons behind her madness. So what do you want me to do?" He looked around the room.

"Oh grab those boxes over there. Don't you want to hear about my job?"

"Yeah...yeah. What sort of job is it?"

"You won't believe this, Randy. This old woman wants me to move into her old rambling house...you know, the one that stands on the hill looking over the beach near La Jolla Shores? The one that is so hidden by trees and plants you can barely see it? Believe it or not, the old lady wants me to find a way into a locked room in that house. She has never been in the room before, and it belonged to her mother, who died when she was born. She is in a wheelchair, has been since she was sixteen, and so she can't go into the room, and the housekeeper, won't let her in anyway. She knows nothing about her mother, and wants me to help her discover something about her. She wants me to figure out a way into the room, by finding the key, hopefully, or maybe by breaking in, if all else fails. Can you believe that she has never even seen a picture of her mother, and her grandparents, who raised her, refused to tell her anything about her? This is a mystery, and I am going to help her find the answers to her past."

"Wow... that is really strange. You sure you want to have that kind of job? What do you know about sleuthing?"

"Only what I have read in Nancy Drew," she admitted. "But don't you think that would be exciting?

"It certainly isn't a typical job. I don't know how you ever managed to land such a strange occupation."

"Because my name is Loraine," she smiled. "Her mother's name was Loraine, and that is the reason she hired me. She didn't even interview me. She just hired me because I had the same name as her mother did."

"She sounds a little loony, I would be careful if I were you," he warned.

"Oh, she is harmless. And I like her. I feel sort of...connected to her in some way, having the same name as her mother, and us both losing our mothers so early in life. Of course, she never knew her father. She doesn't even know who he was. She tells me she is a bastard."

"Sounds just hunky dory! Loraine, this is beginning to sound..."

"And on top of that, she has this doll house..." Loraine

chatted on telling him all about the doll house and the rooms in it matching the rooms of the house, except for the locked room.

By the time she was through, Randy was looking at her quite seriously, with his eyebrows raised.

"I don't know if I should let you accept this job, Rainy. She sounds so exocentric that she may be dangerous."

"She is just a lonely old lady in a wheelchair, is all. Why shouldn't she have someone to entertain her and grant her wishes of learning about her mother, before she dies? I will gladly help her die happy."

"If you say so," he ruffled her hair with one large palm. "I for one am going to miss you. We have had some good times together, you and I."

"Yes, having a crush on your cousin is pretty hard to deal with. Maybe that is why Aunt Mel wants me to leave. She thinks that what we have may get too serious."

He winked down at her. "Oh, if only you were not my cousin…" He leaned over and kissed her on the cheek.

"In England they allow cousins to get married," she said hopefully.

"And you can see what all that inbreeding has done for them," he teased.

"I suppose you are right. I wouldn't want to have any cross-eyed children if I married you…"

"I can't imagine any of your children being cross-eyed. You are too beautiful to have anything but perfect children, even if they were spawned by a close relative." He held her head in his hands and looked down into her bright green eyes. "You are the most beautiful person I have had the pleasure of meeting, and we should stay close friends for the rest of our lives, regardless of who each of us marry."

"Oh, you have just burst my bubble of true love until death do us part," she pouted.

"It *is* true love, Loraine, but only the kind of love brothers and sisters should have. Believe me, if it could be any other way..."

"Yeah, I suppose it is a good thing I am leaving. I think I would try and attack any woman who came and stole you out from under my nose," she admitted.

"Same here, I would have a hard time watching some man capture your heart, which will happen someday, I assure you. I think it is better all the way around, and maybe that is what mother had in mind. She is not blind or stupid, you know." He dropped his hands from her face, and turned to pick up one of the boxes she had indicated.

She pushed the door open for him, and was met by that same grinning face she had left in the kitchen a few minutes earlier, or maybe it was longer than that, she thought.

"Hi. Your aunt sent me up. Said you were taking too dang long…her words, not mine… And I was to help you put your stuff in the basement, and whatever else you needed."

"Just can't wait to get rid of me!" Loraine lamented. "Ok then, grab that box in the corner, and follow Randy. He will show you the way to the basement."

Lawrence picked up the box, and Loraine noticed how his dark hair fell over his forehead in a very attractive way, when he bent to pick it up, and how the muscles in his arms hardened as he lifted it. She was watching him, unabashed, and he looked into her emerald eyes, as he passed, giving her a wink. "Glad to be of some help," he said.

"Yeah, I can see that…" she responded, and went over to grab another small box and followed him down, as Randy led the way.

When all her extra boxes were stowed in the basement, she started on her luggage that she needed to put in her car. Both Randy and Lawrence helped her carry the things out, and stick it in the front trunk of the VW. When they had finished, she gave Randy a hug.

"I am not even going in to say goodbye to Aunt Mel. Tell her thanks for everything, and when I get a place of my own, I will come and get all my things out of her basement. Maybe she will want to rent that out too!"

"You'll cool off in a day or two and come see us," Randy predicted.

"Don't you wish? It will take more than a day or two."

"I hope you do come and see your aunt. I am afraid we got off on the wrong foot, and I would like to get to know you better," Lawrence admitted.

"Humph!" Loraine, growled, "the man who will be sleeping in my bed? In my room...?"

"That sounds enticing, sleeping in your bed..."

"Glad I won't be there to witness it!" she spat.

"Too bad, I would have liked it..."

"Very funny!" She turned and opened the door to her car.

"What, no hug for me?"

"Only reserved for kissing cousins," she smiled, and turned and gave Randy a kiss on the cheek.

"Wow... that was a slap!" Lawrence mumbled.

Loraine only smiled. "Ta ta, as they say in England, where they allow cousins to marry..." She winked at Randy.

"Oh, I see how things were," Lawrence said, as she climbed in and slammed the door.

"Nah, we are just good friends. She uses me to keep all the men at bay. Kind of a protection mechanism, she is so hot, that every man that sees her is always hitting on her. If they think I'm her man, they will keep their distance. It is a game we play, nothing more."

"The protecting cousin, huh?"

"Yeah, and don't you forget it." Randy laughed.

The two watched as the little red VW Bug putted down the road, and then turned the corner disappearing from their view. Lawrence thought the color of her car suited her. She was red hot, and knew it, but like the little Bug she drove, she tried to keep a low profile, while still being noticed by the bright red color.

Randy patted Lawrence on the back. "Don't get any ideas, buster, she is not the girl for you. She has a lot of soul searching to do, before she will ever be ready for a serious relationship, and a one night stand is not going to cut it either, because that is where I will step in."

Lawrence shrugged. "She doesn't like me anyway. After all, I will be sleeping in her bed, in her room...alas without her there to share it."

"Make sure that is how it remains too," Randy warned, and sauntered away, back into the house.

Lawrence shook his head sadly, and followed Randy in. Oh well, he had his own agenda to take care of. As soon as he located his own distant cousin, Amelia Landon, he was going to have to do some fancy talking to get her to consent to his request. He just hoped she hadn't died already, seeing as how she was his only living relative that he was aware of. Hunting her down had not been easy. He hadn't even known she existed until his mother had mentioned the Landon secret that his dad had confided in her shortly before he died. Seems they were distant cousins to a very wealthy family that seemed to have some sort of dark secret. He didn't know what the secret was, except that it had something to do with the granddaughter that no one seemed to know much about. He doubted if she even knew about him either, and so he was curious to find her since she seemed to be his last living relative, and of course filthy rich. Not that he cared about the money, he had his own wealth, but he was curious about the house, which he heard she had been born in, and had been in the family since it was built. He wondered who she was going to leave it to, when she died.

Loraine looked in her rearview mirror and saw Randy and Lawrence/Larry watching her as she drove away. She had to admit to herself that that Lawrence guy was a hunk, and he seemed to be taken by her as well. Isn't that the way things went though? Just as she was starting out on her own, some good looking man moves into her old room, and she probably would not see him again for a long time, seeing as how she was going to keep a low profile and not visit her aunt for a while. She had wanted to start out on her own, but to be pushed out so abruptly by her aunt made her feel like she was unwanted, and it probably had to do with her crush on her cousin. But who could help loving Randy? He was a wonderful guy, and she envied the woman who finally won his heart.

It didn't take long before she approached the house where she was to begin her strange job. She pulled up the steep driveway that led to the back of the house, instead of parking on the street like before. The back of the house was just as overgrown as the front of the house. It was almost like a jungle, considering the palm trees, and banana plants, elephant ears, and bird of paradise, made one believe that some monkeys, or giraffes were going to pop out at any minute.

The VW putted to a stop, and Loraine climbed out of the car, and looked around. Her heart felt light. She was going to like this position very much. She could remain in the house without having to exert herself by taking on any social life, and it would just be her and Amelia, together with the housekeeper/jailor, and a mystery to solve. How she ever managed to find such an ideal position, she would never know, but she thanked the gods that were responsible, and went to the back door, and knocked.

As expected, the housekeeper answered, and told her to bring her things in, and she would show her the room to put them in. Mary Mathews did not seem very happy to have Loraine coming to stay, but she, after all was the hired help, and could not dictate to Amelia what she could do or not do, as long as the locked room remained locked. She looked sideways at the young girl beside her. She spelled trouble, this Mary knew, and she decided she had better keep an eye on her. Young people were so unpredictable, and she would not be surprised if Amelia did not have something up her sleeve, hiring a companion, when she had never requested one before.

On top of that, the girl had the same name as Amelia's mother, and she knew how much Amelia wanted to know about her mother. She felt bad that she was bound to a death bed promise to keep that very information from her. But a promise was a promise, and Mary was a woman of her word. Besides, what good would it do the old woman to learn about her mother at this late date? She had lived her life, what little there was of it, sitting in a wheelchair all day working on that ridicules doll house. And then cluttering the house with all that junk she bought at antique shops or garage sales. The woman was a little addled. She had so much money, she didn't know what to do with it, and since she had no relatives that she knew of, she wondered who she was going to leave all that money to? It certainly would not be her. That Mary knew well. Amelia had never liked her, because she was the one who kept her from her mother's old room.

Even Mary was curious as to what was in that room, but there was no key. She had tried all of her keys, and even the skeleton keys, and nothing opened the door. They would have to remove that door in order to enter the room, and as long as she worked here, that was never going to happen.

She turned and smiled at the girl. "This is your room, she told her, as she pushed the door open to the 'yellow' room.

Loraine took in her breath. She remembered seeing the room in the doll house and thinking what a pretty room it was. It was right next door to the locked room, so Loraine knew why Amelia had put her in it. "Thank you," she said to the house keeper. "When I am unpacked, should I go see Amelia?" she asked.

"Jasper will bring the rest of your things up, but Amelia is resting right now, and then she will have her evening meal in her room, so tomorrow will probably be the earliest that you will be able to see her. Then she will explain all your duties, if she hasn't already."

Mary turned and went back down the hall, and Loraine went into the Yellow room and looked around. The first thing she did was go to the window, because she knew this room faced out on the ocean, and she could not wait to see the view. She pushed the sheer ruffled curtains aside and pulled up the blind. The room filled with sparkling light that illuminated the room making it all the more sunny with its yellow walls, and white spread on the bed, with small yellow rose buds scattered over it. Loraine turned back to the window, and gazed out over the jungle below, and on out to the shore.

The house had its own private beach, which excited Loraine, since she knew she could go there without being disturbed by anyone. The waves crashed and sprayed along the part of the shore that had some rocks jutting out on it. She loved the sound of the crashing waves, and knew she could not bear to live any place away from the ocean. It was in her blood. The salt smell, the sand, and shells, and seaweed. The tide coming in and going out, bringing surprises up to the shore for her to discover the next morning. The feel of power that the ocean owned, something she lacked, but that she felt buoy her up when she needed a lift. Walking along the shore soothed her, and she knew that living here would give her a chance to take advantage of that need to feel the wet sand under her feet and hear the seagulls scream overhead, and feel the spray of salt water against her face, when the wind blew it off of the waves.

She stood for a very long time watching the waves, in hypnotic stance as though they pulled her to them. In them was a secret she knew nothing about, but as she stood in that room, she felt something strangely familiar, as though she had seen this view before, a Deja Vu sort of feeling, and she felt a shiver go through her. And something else strange took over her. She was seeing the face of Lawrence in her mind, but he was not dressed as he had been when she met him. He seemed to have old fashion clothes on, early turn of the century, she thought. How odd. Whatever made her think of him in such a get up? Was it romance? She had always thought that era was romantic. Perhaps that was what it was, she thought, as she turned to her luggage, and started unpacking her things.

CHAPTER THREE

The sun shone into the yellow room, almost blinding Loraine, when she opened her eyes. She realized that she had not closed the blind, and now the room was full of morning sunshine that danced on the ancient wall paper, of large yellow roses. It seemed as though the buds on the bedspread had suddenly bloomed and took their place climbing up the wall like an invisible trellis. The white dresser, trimmed in yellow, braced itself against the wall, as the mirror tilted at just the right angle for Loraine to see her reflection in it.

There she sat among the pile of pillows around her, the lacy bedspread rumpled about her, the gauze of the white draping from the canopy above her head swaying lightly in the breeze from the open window; her eyes wide as she stared at her reflection with her long sandy hair draped about her shoulders. Green flecks danced in her eyes as she glanced about the room and realized that she now lived in this house... the house that had always drawn her as a child.

She had been told by her school chums that a witch lived in that house and she was never to go near it. Their parents had warned them it was dangerous, which made it all the more attractive to Loraine, who had an imaginative mind and wouldn't mind meeting a witch or two. But of course, Amelia was no witch. She was just a lonely woman, trapped in her wheelchair in the house that she obsessed on, with doll house copies, and filling with objects which really meant nothing to her, since they were not part of her past, or belonged to any members of her family.

Loraine pushed the blankets back from the bed and alighted on one of the plush yellow throw rugs that was placed at either side of the bed, covering a larger area rug of intricate design in a combination of yellow, pinks, light green and white. Her bare feet sank into it, as though they were sinking into the soft sand of the beach. A rocker sat idle on the other side of the dresser, painted white and yellow, with the same design in the trim as the dresser, and a cushion to match the bedspread. The curtains also matched the bedspread with little yellow rose buds climbing up their edges.

Loraine pushed her feet into her slippers, and padded over to the closet, where she had put her clothes, and pulled out a soft flowing sun dress, which was also yellow. It seemed like a yellow day to her, and she decided to keep it that way. Her heart was light and bright, and she was starting on a new adventure. The spaghetti strapped dress showed off her even tan, and her hair falling down like a wave of water, streaked by the sun, rested on her shoulders like a veil of netting, accentuating her tan.

After examining herself in the mirror to make sure that she

was presentable, she turned to the door, and started down the steps. She wasn't sure about breakfast, or where it would be served, so she decided to hunt up the housekeeper, which was not difficult, as she was standing in the entrance hall, when Loraine reached it, by one of the double stair cases that wound on either side of the entrance hall.

"Amelia is waiting for you in the same room, where you were interviewed," Mary informed her, as she approached her.

Loraine smiled. It was not much of an interview, but she had certainly learned a lot about her employer. Much more than Amelia had learned about herself during that so called interview. She went to the door, and put her hand on the knob, pushing the door in. As she did, she saw Amelia in her wheelchair, smiling and apparently talking to someone in the room, which Loraine could not see. She entered the room, and saw the back of a tall dark headed man, looking down at the doll house, his hand resting on the corner of it, as he examined the inside with great interest. Lorain knew he was not Jasper. This man was young with a good build and broad shoulders, not hunched over like the handy man.

"Oh, there you are Loraine," Amelia turned to acknowledge Loraine as she stepped into the room, "I want you to meet my distant cousin. Imagine, I actually have someone related to me! I didn't even know about him until this morning, when he showed up on my doorstep!"

As she spoke, the man turned, and Loraine felt as though she had become stone. She could not move. She only stared. As she took in the man that stood before her, she thought he was dressed in that same outfit she had envisioned him wearing the night before, when she was looking out her window. Then her vision cleared, and she could see Lawrence standing there, grinning at her in the same surprise that she was staring at him with.

"Loraine, I would like you to meet Lawrence Bradley Landon my cousin three times removed, whatever that means. He claims that I am his only living relative, and has had a heck of a time trying to hunt me down. Imagine that?"

Loraine shook the shock from her shoulders, by shaking her head back and forth, causing her hair to flow about her shoulders in a sunlight dance. Lawrence's grin broadened as he watched her hair flow about her, one eyebrow raised, and a quizzical gleam in his dark eyes.

Finally Loraine managed to speak. "Oh... Larry!" She gave him a mischievous smile. "He is the man who so rudely moved into my room almost before I had a chance to move out!" She looked him up and down. "Are you sure he is your cousin, Amelia? I don't think I would trust him, if I were you!"

"Larry? You know this man?"

"No, not really, I just met him yesterday. My aunt calls

him Larry, though."

"I assure you, my name is Lawrence, and no one, other than your aunt, has ever called me Larry!" His eyes sizzled at Loraine.

"Well, well, please do tell me your story, Larry...oh yes, excuse me... Lawrence Bradley Landon. I am all ears. After all, I have been hired as this woman's companion, and I plan to protect her from uninvited characters who claim to be related to her. Everyone knows she is worth a fortune, and I for one, will persuade her from leaving her money to some upstart that pretends to be her cousin, or any other distant relative just on his say so."

Amelia's eyes widened. "Thank you dear. I knew I could trust you to be loyal. Perhaps you could repeat your story to my young companion here. I will have her check you out...if that is the right expression."

"She can check me out any day," Lawrence drawled. "Do all the checking you want, *Ranie*"

"Oh, you heard Randy call me that! Don't you ever use that name for me again. It is reserved for close friends and dear cousins!"

"You mean kissing cousins?" he teased.

Loraine could not keep the blush from spreading over her face. She could strangle the man! How dare he!

She swallowed hard to maintain her temper, and said calmly, "My relationship to my cousin is no concern of yours, apparently, Randy has found it entertaining to relate to you something, which you have taken out of context, and…"

"If I remember right, *you* are the one who called him your kissing cousin," he interrupted.

"I was joking!" she fumed, as her eyes narrowed and sparked at him.

"Whoa, don't shoot me with daggers from those flaming green eyes of yours, it will hit me right in the heart, and I will have to confess my never dying love for you!"

Amelia watched with amused eyes, at the little confrontation. She was beginning to like both of these young people very much. They were starting to turn her dull life into something more exciting and enjoyable. She did not interrupt them because she was enjoying the exchange.

"Don't you wish?" Loraine responded to his tease. "I am not interested in what kind of feelings you pretend to have for me. I am only interested in what kind of cock and bull story you are trying to get Amelia to believe. So go ahead, inform me of your claims, so I can 'check you out'!" As she said the last three words, she scanned her eyes over him from head to toe, and then gave him a disarming smile. "So far, I don't see much!"

"Okay, okay, little miss. For your information, I *am* related to Amelia Loraine Landon."

"You didn't tell me your middle name was Loraine!" She

turned to Amelia, her eyes with surprise.

"It was the name my mother gave me before she died, but my Grandfather refused to ever use my middle name. We never mentioned my middle name."

"Oh..." This information took her back a bit, and she looked a little less sure of herself, as she drew her gaze back to Lawrence. "Go ahead, tell us your fabricated story," she said with a little less conviction.

"Not fabricated. The truth! The Landons had distant relatives in New York. The shoe factory started there, before the brother of the New York Landons moved to California and built up the business there. The two brothers were never close, and were always in competition of each other, even though it was the family business. When the California business started going under, the brother of Amelia's grandfather, sent his son out to see if he could straighten things out. His son disappeared, and his brother claimed the young man, had been there with his sister, but left shortly after his sister sailed with her future husband. The California end of the business went bankrupt, and the New York end refused to help, and disowned that branch of the family, believing they were responsible for the boy's disappearance. They sent investigators but could never solve the mystery of the missing son. They did discover that the boy did show up, but no one knew what happened to him after that.

"He was their only son, and the mother of the boy pined away and died of a broken heart. By the way, the missing boy's name was Lawrence, so I am told. Anyway, his father remarried and had another son, and that son was my great, grandfather. Anyway, to make a long story short, that makes me a cousin three times removed, to Amelia, and since both my mother and father are dead, and there are no other cousins to clutter things up, she and I are the last of the line….so to speak. I just thought it would be proper to discover the only living relative I have left in this world. I heard a lot about the house, which was designed by the Landon who came to California originally to set up the business. I wanted to see it. After my great grandfather's half-brother disappeared, no one spoke of the California family, but claimed there was some secret involving them, most likely how my great uncle had disappeared. I did not know of this family secret, or any of this, until after my own father died, because he never told my mother until right before he died, and then she told me. So I decided to come and investigate."

"Well, it looks like we have two mysteries on our hands," Amelia stated. "Why my grandfather hated my mother, and what happened to the cousin who never returned home."

Lawrence looked questioningly at Amelia.

"That is why I hired this sweet girl, the one you must confess your undying love to…" she chuckled. "I want her to discover why my grandfather locked my mother's room, and then never spoke of her again, not even to me. Perhaps you can be of some help as well, seeing as how you are trying to discover what happened to your great uncle, whom my grandfather claimed left right after his sister left. By the way, my grandfather was Hennery Malcolm Landon, and his wife's name was Loretta May Bradley Landon."

"Strange. Bradley was the maiden name of my great, great grandfather's first wife who was the mother of the young man who disappeared. That is where I got my middle name. I wonder if the two were sisters."

"Could be, who knows, I have never done any research into my family, seeing as how I don't even know who my real father is," Amelia said sadly. "But now I want to know everything, and how exciting to find someone who knows something about the family history."

"Okay, then, truce?" he asked Loraine, as he put out his hand.

"Not until you can prove you are actually who you say you are," she insisted.

"Will a driver's license work, or do you need my birth certificate?" he grinned.

He handed her his driver's license and she looked down at it. Unless it was a forgery, he seemed to be who he said he was.

Loraine did not think he would go to the trouble to forge a driver's license just to prove his relationship to this woman.

"Oh, and by the way," he added. "I am not after my cousin's money. I was a member of the side of the family who were successful in the business, after the California end went under. I have plenty of money of my own. In fact you might call me independently wealthy, and that is why I have the time to investigate this mystery. Not to mention, it would cause me great pleasure if I could sort of help put this place back to its former glory. My major in college was architecture, and I love landscaping as well. If you would let me, I could put this place back in shape for you, Cousin Amelia." He gave her a reassuring smile, one that Loraine realized that few could resist.

"I had planned to let the house die with me," Amelia admitted, "But now…it seems only right to restore it. Heaven knows, I can afford it, and having young people around the place, seems to call for something less run down than this old place is. Yes, if it can assure young people like you will remain here to keep me company, I will gladly let you be in charge of restoring the place."

"Well you have certainly put your foot in the door," Loraine said to Lawrence, as she witnessed his satisfied smirk.

"Looks like we both have our foot in the door," he retorted, "And a beautiful foot you have too!" He looked down at Loraine's sandaled foot with painted pink toenails.

"You just keep your toes off of my feet. No stumbling around trying to lead this dance!"

"Oh, you dance too? How charming?"

"You know what I mean. You just stay to your own business. And by the way, how do you like my room?"

"Oh, if you could only know what keeps going through my mind, while I sleep in your bed, in your room...."

"Sorry I asked."

Amelia smiled at the two. This was going to work out just fine, she thought. She was sure they were both attracted to each other, but just wouldn't admit it, and what could be more exciting than a sparkling love affair, unfolding right under her nose, in her house? Oh how she wished she were younger!

CHAPTER FOUR

After her confrontation with Lawrence, Loraine ate her breakfast in the kitchen, while Lawrence and Amelia continued to visit in the front parlor. As she was leaving the kitchen, she saw Lawrence at the front door, on his way out. She came up behind him and tapped him on the shoulder, causing him to jump.

"Damn, do you have to scare me out of my wits?" he growled at her as he spun around, seeing it was her.

"What's the matter? Do you think there are ghosts in this house?" she countered.

"It is probably full of them, after the story that Amelia told me about her mother and all, and the disappearance of my great uncle, or whoever he was, I wouldn't be surprised if this place is haunted."

"Sorry to disappoint you, but I am not a ghost, of Christmas-past, or Christmas-future, I just wanted to ask you a question."

"Okay, shoot!"

"Wouldn't I like to, but I haven't a gun handy right at this moment."

He laughed, and she noticed how the lines around his eyes

crinkled, and his mouth curved in a most attractive way. "What did I ever do to earn your disdain?"

"Oh, I suppose it was not your fault that you moved into my room, while I was practically still in it, so I forgive you."

"I wish you *had* still been in it. You would make a delightful bed partner." He gave her a long sizzling look.

"Don't push your luck! I am not available. I am madly in love with my kissing cousin."

"Oh, he told me about how you use him to keep the men at bay. What are you so afraid of?"

"Are you expecting me to pour my little 'ol' heart out to you, and tell you my deep dark secrets? Sorry pal, I don't even know you."

"I hope to remedy that!"

"But until then, I need to know if you can get a key made for that locked room?"

"Well, I don't know. I would have to see what kind of lock it is. Let's go take a look."

She led the way, and Lawrence followed her, as he took in the sway of her hips, and how her hair waved around her body, when she climbed the stairs in front of him. How he would like to put his hands on those luscious looking hips… He tried to distract his thoughts, by looking at the pictures on the wall of the hall, when they reached the landing.

"This is it. I have the yellow room next door, and next door to that is the blue room, and then across the hall there is the red room...."

"A regular artist's pallet, huh? I think people liked to do that in the old days, so they could keep track of who was sleeping in what room," he chuckled. "So this is the infamous room you are to break into? They don't make these kinds of locks anymore, you know, but you can usually find a skeleton key that fits them."

"Where do you think we can get one?"

"Off of the housekeeper? After all she would have to get into all the rooms to take care of them. In the old days they had one key that they could use to fit most of the locks, so the housekeeper or maids had access to the rooms in order to clean them and such."

"Well I don't think the housekeeper is going to offer us a key. Amelia did mention to you that she has sworn to keep that door locked, until the day she or Amelia dies, whichever comes first."

"Hmmm, seems the only solution is to swipe the key from her. Do you know where she keeps them?"

"I have only been here one day, but I am sure she guards them with her life."

"Not necessarily. After all, Amelia is in a wheelchair, and even if she got the key, she couldn't get upstairs to unlock the door, so why would Miss Mathews worry about the key being taken?"

"That is true, but since I don't know where she keeps them at the moment, I will have to wait until I do find out. Guess I will have to figure this out later. In the meantime, I think I will pay a visit to the local library, and look up some things about the Landons and see if they are mentioned in the society pages of the newspaper of their day."

"Smart move, I am going to start on the outside of this house. Doesn't look like Amelia has had a gardener take shears to anything for a very long time, and that handyman, is not very handy, so she informs me. He is probably here for a free ride, if you ask me."

"You are probably right."

"Well, I can't do anything to the outside of the house, such as painting and repairing fascia, or trim, and whatnot, until the jungle is tamed."

"I can't wait to see how it looks when you are finished. I remember this house from my childhood, and it has always looked this way."

"Then things are going to change around here. Amelia said she would get me some photographs of the house in its hay day, so I can see how things looked then. Maybe we can find a happy medium between then and now."

"Sounds like a winner, but I gotta go, if I am going to get anything done."

She turned and tripped down the stairs in a sort of high energy skip, and Lawrence admired the bounce of her yellow skirt, which revealed well shaped calves and ankles. For a moment, he envisioned her dressed in the same era that the house was built in. She would have fit there perfectly, he thought, but she wouldn't be bouncing down the stairs like she was, he realized, as he shook his head and the vision faded.

Loraine could feel his eyes on her, and she gave a little mischievous smile, and then she thought about his question of what she was afraid of? That puzzled her. She had not had any heart breaking relationships, or had even been in love, as far as she could remember, unless she was blocking something out, she laughed to herself. The only man she ever felt any attraction to was her cousin, and that was not a mad love affair, so what *was* she afraid of? It seemed that as long as she could remember, she had feared falling in love with anyone. She was afraid it would end badly, but she didn't know why she had that feeling, since she hadn't had a bad experience with love or losing someone she loved, or being left flat by someone? It was just an inner feeling that always seemed to be there.

Sure, she had those romantic thoughts of finding the perfect love and getting married, like all girls did, but the moment she thought someone actually was starting to like her, or tried to get to know her better, she suddenly felt a panic, and just treated them flippantly, to keep them at a distance. She hadn't even let anyone kiss her seriously, except for that one time, when she kissed Randy, but they both realized that was a big mistake, the moment it happened. So now he helped her keep the men at arm's length, and she tried not to think about it. It was fun having Randy as a friend, because it kept her from having to deal with a boyfriend. And that suited her just fine. If she wanted to go out on the town, or dancing, Randy would gladly take her.

Now she was afraid that Lawrence was going to try and tear down her well established barrier that always kept men at a distance. There was something about him. Some sort of determination that she was going to have to keep an eye on. She was sure he wanted to tame her, in the same way he planned to tame the jungle growing around the house. What was so maddening was that he was so good looking it hurt to look at him! Her heart was always in a flutter, when he flirted with her, and she had to stay on her toes in order to keep one step ahead of him to deflect his charm and his piercing dark eyes. And that smile. That smile was something to die for! No, she was not going to fall at his feet, no matter how hard he tried to persuade her. No one had gotten that close to her yet, and she was determined not to allow it to happen now. Not in this life time anyway, she resolved.

She went to the back of the house, and climbed into her VW. She noticed the brand new shinny green BMW parked alongside of her car. Well Lawrence must have money, like he claimed. She realized that he probably figured that she must work there, when he saw her car in the drive. After all, he had helped her put her things in the trunk and knew that someone had hired her, where she was to be a live in help, and if he wasn't dumb he would have put two and two together, as soon as he saw her car. Strange that the very man who came to take over her bedroom at her aunt's house, was now there trying to take over her heart, in the very place she was working. Damn! She would have to see him every day! How was she ever going to continue to keep her distance from him?

This was not going to be as easy as blowing off some guy at a dance that flirted with her, or some friend that was getting too personal, whom she could just stop seeing any more. She was going to have to work in the same surroundings as he did, and he had a vested interest in discovering the history of the family, even more than she did. After all she was a stranger to Amelia and the family. He was a distant relative. That meant he would probably want her to keep him up to date on everything she managed to discover. What had she ever gotten herself into? She shook her head. Oh well. She would just have to take it a day at a time.

Loraine pulled the little red bug into the parking lot of the local library, and found a space to park. She had pulled her hair back out of her way by tying a scarf around her head, and then tying the ends around her hair as she pulled it back into a long ponytail. She knew her hair was what seemed to attract men, so when she was in public, and didn't want to be bothered by them hitting on her, she tried to keep it covered and contained. She absently pulled the long strip of hair over her shoulder, and started to braid it, then fastened a rubber band at the end and threw it back over her shoulder to make a long queue down her back.

Now she jauntily stepped into the library and went to the microfilm section of old newspapers, and looked in the ones that were eighty years old, or older. It didn't take her long to find something written about the Landons. It seemed that Amelia's mother had been engaged, about a year before Amelia was born. Apparently she had not married the man, or Amelia would have had a father, whom she knew, and even if she was a bastard, she would have had a man who thought he was her father, or took the place of her father. She read the article.

Mr. and Mrs. Landon proudly announces the engagement of their daughter, Loraine Marie Landon to Gaston Michael Billings, the date of the marriage, yet to be announced.

There was no photograph of either of them, and Loraine wondered what had happened, since obviously, the two did not get married? Had her mother been jilted, after she discovered she was pregnant? Was that why Amelia was a bastard? She wanted to discover who this Gaston Billings was, and why they did not end up getting married? After all Amelia's last name was Landon, not Billings. She continued to search the microfilm, and discovered that Gaston Billings was a prominent man in the area who was president of the local bank. He was a widower, which meant that he was probably a lot older than Loraine was, unless he was widowed at a young age. But men did not become presidents of banks when they were in their youth, she figured. She wondered if Loraine was in love with the banker, regardless of their age difference. Or maybe Loraine was older, a spinster, who finally found true love, and something messed it up?

She continued to search the clippings after the engagement announcement and found the answer.

Mysterious disappearance of Loraine Landon is yet to be solved. Loraine Landon, who was to be married to Gaston Billings, did not appear at St. John's Church on her wedding day. The guests and wedding party were concerned when the bride did not appear to take the hand of her husband at the altar. Mrs. Landon was the last person to see her daughter, claiming that the bride had put her gown on and was ready to leave the house, but when Mrs. Landon came to the room again, she could not find her daughter, nor could they discover her in the house either. The grounds were searched, and the surrounding area. There was no sign of the girl, and it was not until later that Mrs. Landon discovered that the wedding gown her daughter had been wearing was still in her room, hung neatly in her wardrobe, which meant the bride had removed the gown herself, and was either abducted, or she left on her own. The daughter did not leave any note of explanation, nor was there any ransom note demanding money either. The family is still searching for their daughter, and hope to discover the answer to the mystery of why she did not attend her own wedding.

Apparently they had found the daughter, because she came back to give birth to Amelia, Loraine reasoned. But what had happened to her, and why did she never get married to the banker? She continued to search the newspaper, and discovered that after several days, they did find Loraine, but refused to make any comment to the newspaper. The wedding had been called off.

This told Loraine nothing, so she had to find a way into the room. She hoped that Amelia was right and that Loraine had kept a diary, because that would probably reveal the answers. She made copies of the newspaper clippings, and stuffed them in her purse. At least she had this much to show Amelia, and that was a start.

Loraine clattered into the entrance way, eager to show Amelia the little bit that she had found about her mother. She almost ran head long into Lawrence, and he grabbed her arm to stop her from falling over.

"Why are you always determined to run me down?" he asked, laughing.

"Why are you always in my way? I thought you were going to work in the yard all day?"

"I had to eat. It is lunch time, in case you didn't notice."

"Oh, so it is. Okay. What you got there?" She nodded at the large manila envelope he had in his hand.

"It's pictures of the house, back in the day. This place was pretty swanky back then. When you have some time, come out and look at them. I gotta get back to my taming of the jungle."

"Okay. I need to show Amelia what I found at the library."

"You found something? Anything interesting?"

"If you think jilting your groom at the altar is interesting, then yes."

"This, I gotta hear. Mind if I tag along while you tell her?"

"I am sure you will find out eventually, so be my guest."

He gave her a disarming grin, and put his hand on her elbow, as he followed her into the front parlor.

"You wait here, I will tell Miss Mathews to have Amelia meet us here," she instructed.

He nodded, and she went in search of Miss Mathews. She did not want to disturb Amelia, if she was resting or anything, so she would leave it up to the housekeeper to bring her. When she went into Miss Mathews little office, she noticed a ring of keys hanging on the side of a shelf above her desk. She made a mental note of it, thinking it was probably what she was looking for. Mary Mathews had been sitting at the desk, when Loraine knocked. She shoved her novel into a draw and brought out some papers onto her desk and invited whoever was at the door in. When she saw it was Loraine, she gave a little frown.

"What do you want?" she asked, not too kindly.

"I just wanted to talk to Miss Amelia," Loraine told her.

"She just had lunch and may be resting, but I will see if she wants to talk to you or not."

"Thank you."

"We saved some lunch for you. It's in the frig on a covered tray when you are ready for it."

"That was thoughtful. I will eat it when I am through talking to Miss Amelia."

Loraine turned and left the room, and went back to the parlor to join Lawrence. He gave her a welcoming smile. "Sunshine has just entered the room," he said and then began to sing, "Sunshine on my shoulder makes me happy…" an old John Denver song, and she gave him a shove, pushing him onto the couch with a plop. She sat in one of the green chairs, as they waited for Amelia to appear.

Shortly, the door opened and Amelia wheeled herself into

the room, closing the door behind her. "You wanted to talk to me?" she asked, a little anxiously. "Did you find anything at the library of interest?"

"Well, I discovered that your mother was set to marry a banker, but on the day of the wedding, she took her wedding dress off and disappeared. They didn't know if she left on her own accord, or if someone abducted her. I think she left on her own accord, because when they found her again, the wedding was called off. What do you think about that? Here are copies of the newspaper clippings." She handed them to Amelia, as Lawrence looked on, over her shoulder.

"I guess that means that I am still illegitimate, as my grandfather claimed," Amelia sighed. "When you said she was going to get married, it sort of gave me hope."

"I'm sorry. I wish I had better news, but I am not going to give up. We will get to the bottom of this. I saw where the housekeeper keeps her keys, and I plan to see if she has one to the room, or if a skeleton key might fit the lock."

"That is promising," Amelia murmured, as she looked over the newspaper articles in her hand.

"Maybe I should help you get into that room," Lawrence offered.

"Why? If I have a key, I don't need your help."

"Moral support?" he suggested with a sly grin.

"I don't need moral support. You tend to your taming of the jungle, and I will do my sleuthing on my own, thank you very much."

"I have a feeling you are not eager for my company."

"How'd you ever guess?"

"Okay. Okay. I can take a hint. I'm outa here." He got up and headed for the door. "But don't forget to tell me what you find, if you do get into that room. After all I am the distant relative, not you."

"Yeah... yeah, if you say so."

Loraine left Amelia, reading the clippings she had given her, and went to the kitchen to eat the lunch they had saved for her. As she walked towards the kitchen, she removed the scarf, and undid her braid, shaking her hair free, as she pushed the kitchen door open. She didn't realize how famished she was until she sat down and started eating the ham sandwich that had been made for her. She guzzled down the orange juice, and took the small bag of potato chips with her. When she passed Mary Mathews in the hall, she made an about face, and headed back to the woman's office, opened the door, grabbed the ring of keys off of the hook, and made a beeline up to the locked room.

Loraine's hands shook, as she tried each key that looked like it might fit, into the key hole on the door. When none of the keys turned the lock, not even the skeleton key, she tried them all again, but with no luck. Either the Housekeeper kept that key someplace else, or that key did not exist and not even the housekeeper could open the door. Now Loraine did not know what she could do to open the door, since not even the skeleton key seemed to open it. She decided to go talk to Lawrence about it, and see if he had any ideas.

Loraine took the keys back and placed them on their hook, and began eating the potato chips as she went back down the hall. As much as it galled her to have to approach Lawrence, and ask his opinion, she had no other choice. She headed out the back door, and followed the sound of music, blaring from the radio out into the back yard. Lawrence was working on plants that surrounded a large patio that had a huge birdbath in the center of it. There were even wild vines winding themselves around the birdbath, not to mention several large pots placed about the patio that were full of plants as well.

Lawrence did not hear her approach, seeing as how the music was so loud she wondered that it didn't break his ear drums. She stood and watched him for a while, as she ate the potato chips. His back was to her, and he was dancing and clipping the hedge at the same time. She had to muffle her laughs, so he didn't hear her, as she watched him sway his shoulders and move his hips to the disco music that filled the air, as he made exaggerated clips and leaves went flying. He did a little turn, and when he did, he saw her there. Without missing a beat, he flung the clippers aside, grabbed her hand, removing the bag of potato chips, and tossed them, then pulled her into the dance with him. They were both laughing so hard that neither of them could manage the steps. He grabbed her waist and did a couple of tango steps with her, ending with her bent backwards against his arm, and him leaning over her, his face inches from hers.

Before she realized it, he had leaned in and captured her mouth with his. She stiffened, but then his hand that had been holding her hand, dropped her hand and took its place at the nap of her neck, holding her head against his mouth, so he could complete the kiss, which pulled a strange passion from the pit of Loraine's stomach. When he finally pulled his lips from hers, she felt breathless, and then angry, as she jerked away, and glared at him.

"You have a lot of nerve...!" she began.

"Sure do. Gotta catch you when you least expect it. I doubt you would ever give me permission to kiss you, and you looked like you needed kissing. I couldn't help myself!"

"I didn't come out here to get mauled by you."

"You are a great dancer. Has anyone told you? And you can actually tango! Imagine that! We should hit all the hot spots."

"In your dreams, buddy!"

"Awe, don't be like that. I'm a swell guy. I could show you a great time. You just need to get rid of that chip on your shoulder."

"What is on my shoulder is none of your business."

He stepped towards her, smiling. "I mean that potato chip that is on your shoulder, he laughed, as he brushed it off. "Now that is better."

Loraine frowned. He was always teasing her, and she never knew when to take him seriously.

"Okay, you had your fun. But whether you are a swell guy or not, I am not looking for a good time, and I only came out here to see those pictures you told me about, and to get your opinion on something." His face brightened. "Don't start thinking I like you just because I need you to suggest something to me," she added when she saw the look on his face.

"You sure know how to make my day," he grinned. "Okay, beautiful, what can I do for you? If you don't think of something, I can suggest a lot of things…"

"None of the keys fit," she said, cutting him off, "not even the skeleton key."

"What a bummer! You sure? Skeleton keys usually do the trick."

"I tried them twice. Now what should we try?"

"I don't know. Maybe I could try climbing the trellis that is outside the window. Hope it is not all rotted."

"Yeah, why don't you try it? It faces the back. No one will

see you."

"Okay, gorgeous, but only on the condition, that you will give me a real kiss. If I am going to break my neck, I want to at least have one good memory before I die."

"Do I detect blackmail?" Loraine narrowed her eyes.

"Call it what you wish, but I am not taking one step up that trellis until you allow me to kiss you without you pushing me away or slapping my face. And the duration of the kiss has to be left up to me." He gave her an evil grin.

Loraine paused and thought about it.

"Don't take all day. We're burning daylight here."

"Oh!" Loraine growled between her teeth. "Oh…okay, have at it, but I don't have to enjoy this!"

Lawrence's face stretched into a full grin, and Loraine noticed he had a dimple in one cheek, which she hadn't noticed before. She couldn't keep her eyes off of it, and it made her heart take a little jump, when she saw how appealing it looked to her.

"That's a good sign," Lawrence whispered, as he caught the look on her face, and she immediately straightened her expression. He moved in closer, and looked into her eyes, just gazing into them, with a serious look on his face.

"What are you waiting for? I said I would let you kiss me."

"I know, I know, but let me do this my way, okay?"

"Your way will take all day."

"Hmmm, good idea." He was still looking into her eyes, and then his eyes searched her face, and landed on her mouth. Loraine's mouth gave a small impatient twitch, which caused Lawrence to grin at her, and that made her grin as well, as the dimple appeared unexpectedly.

In the middle of her grinning at him, his head bent and his mouth captured her smiling mouth, which was half open, and slowly, his tongue licked lightly against that smile, causing her to catch her breath. He continued the alarming kiss, and she was not stopping him. She couldn't stop him, or he would not climb the trellis, she told herself. She felt his arms pulling her closer, as his fingers raked through her long hair, holding her head steady as he applied more pressure with his lips.

Lawrence pulled her body closer his, with the hand he had against her back. Slowly, his kiss deepened even more, and Loraine found herself responding to the kiss, completely against her will, or was it? She wasn't sure. She only knew that the kiss made her toes curl, and her heart speed to a gallop, and her legs feel like they wouldn't support her, if he let go of her. And strangely, she was melting into him, putting her arms around his neck and clinging on for dear life, as she felt the kiss seep into her very being, and tug at her heart in a way she had never experienced before. Of course, she had never experienced it before. She had never let a man kiss her like this, before! This was something completely new to Loraine, and she wondered what she had been missing all those times she kept holding men off?

Lawrence, could not believe how good she felt in his arms. Her lips were soft and warm and yielding. He felt her hands creep up to his neck, tightening her grip, as he pulled her closer, and tasted her lips. She tasted salty from the potato chips she had been eating, and yet she tasted sweet as well. She was wearing something. Some sent that he couldn't quite recognize, even though it seemed familiar to him, somehow. All he knew was that he loved the smell of it, and he loved the taste of her, and he wanted this kiss to last forever, since it was probably the only one he would ever get from her. He planned to make it worth his while, since he had her where he wanted her, at the moment.

As Lawrence kissed her, he gently pushed her farther into the shrubbery, in case anyone happened to come out and cut the kiss short, and she followed his steps as though in a dance, him pressing forward, and her stepping backward, until they were under the shelter of the ferns and palms, which shaded them. The kiss progressed, as he slanted his head to better accommodate her mouth, and he sucked her lower lip into his mouth, nibbling on it, and then running his tongue across it in tantalizing slowness. He heard a soft groan escape her lips, giving him hope.

Loraine was lost in the kiss. She couldn't understand why she was allowing this, except for the fact that it felt so good, she never wanted him to stop. She should be ashamed of herself, she thought, but she pushed the thought aside, and reveled in the tingling that was starting to scorch her body, at the intenseness which caused her heart to beat faster. He had said he got to decide on the duration of the kiss, but now it didn't seem to matter, because she didn't want to pull away. He could choose to have the kiss last forever, and it wouldn't make any difference, she thought. She would allow it. She wanted it, if it made her feel this way. What other feelings could he pull from her, she wondered? She felt him pulling her trembling body with him as he slowly lowered her to the soft grass, without interrupting the kiss.

Loraine sank down against Lawrence, knowing he was taking advantage of the situation, but now, her heart strangely yearned for something she didn't understand. It was almost as if she had felt this same feeling before, only, how could she, since she had never let anyone kiss her like this before? Somehow it felt natural for her to be in his arms like this. She almost felt dizzy as she felt him clutch her to him, the kiss taking over her senses. It was like she was being transported into another space and time. She wanted to fly away with the feeling that was taking over all rational, causing her breath to come even faster, as his kiss became more demanding.

Finally, Lawrence's lips broke away, and she gasped, either in pleasure or disappointment, he didn't know which. But she didn't say anything, so he captured her lips again, more gently, and coaxing, as she started to relax in his arms and her breathing slowed. He lay for a moment with her still in his arms, at the end of the kiss.

"Thank you for the kiss," he whispered in her ear, as he kissed her lobe, and then moved to her mouth again.

"I...I think that was a little more than just a kiss," she gulped, and then met his renewed kiss.

"Do you want to keep going?" he questioned as he tore his mouth away from hers.

"That would be cheating. You said a kiss, and you got more than just a simple kiss, so don't push your luck."

"Didn't you like it?" He looked into her eyes for the true answer.

"It is not that I didn't like it. I...I just don't want this to go any farther. I thought you only meant a simple kiss. You are just trying to makes me forget my resolve to keep you at arm's length, as handsome as your arms may be," she accused.

"Oh, keeping me at arm's length is just fine with me, as long as the arm's length is close enough to touch you and kiss you like this." He brushed a kiss across her forehead.

"I let you kiss me, so you would help me get into that room. I did not intend to start a love affair with it. It was only supposed to be a kiss... a simple, innocent kiss. You took gross advantage of me, and you know it!"

"I didn't feel you backing away, or screaming no," he reminded her.

"I know. I have no excuse. I just must be wanton, but I intend to correct that in the future."

"No, you are a very enticing and beautiful girl that I would like to hold in my arms all day, if I could."

"I think you have more in mind than just holding me in your arms," Loraine accused.

"Oh, you can read my mind!"

"Okay. You got your kiss, so I hope you are satisfied. Just don't let it happen again. This was only a business arrangement."

"Business arrangement, my ass!"

"I think you are reading too much into it," she said as she sat up. "So forget it. I think it's time you try to climb the trellis and see if you can get into that room."

"All right, but you can't blame me for trying." He rose to his feet and pulled her up, planting a kiss on her nose as she stood before him. "To the trellis," he laughed, as he led the way.

Loraine followed, thinking how handsome he looked, in his tight jeans, and tee shirt that revealed his rippling muscles. She had underestimated him with that kiss. Next time she would be smarter, she reprimanded herself.

CHAPTER FIVE

Lawrence and Loraine, rounded the corner of the house, and stared up the trellis that was overgrown with roses. Lawrence looked at Loraine, a pucker of doubt on his forehead.

"Do you see those roses?" he complained. She nodded. "Did you see the thorns on those roses?" he emphasized. "I may kill myself just climbing up there, getting snagged by all those thorns! Maybe I should demand another kiss…"

"Oh shut up! No more kisses or any other kind of blackmail. You said you would climb the trellis, I kissed you, and now you have to follow through."

"If I don't break my neck I will get scratched to death. Those roses look lethal!"

"Put your gloves on. Don't you have a long sleeved shirt you can put on over your tee shirt?"

"I have a jacket in my car. I'll go get it, and you can look at those pictures, while you're waiting. They're sitting on the picnic table out where I was working."

Loraine followed him back to the place where he was working, and he went around to the driveway to his car. Loraine pulled the pictures from the envelope, and gazed down at them.

Suddenly an extraordinary feeling crept into her. She couldn't stop staring at the house, the way it looked almost a hundred years ago. She knew she had never seen the house like that before, but it looked so familiar to her. She closed her eyes and shook her head to clear it. That kiss must have done something to her brain, she thought, as she opened her eyes again, and stared down at the photograph. Her ears seemed to be ringing, and she could almost feel herself walking up the stairs to the front door, with those same neatly cared for plants surrounding her, and the fresh painted trim, and clean brick and rock walls welcoming her. She was brought out of her daze when she felt Lawrence put his hand on her shoulder.

"What do you think?" he asked, pointing to the pictures in her hand.

"The place looked great back then," she said slowly.

"You okay? You look a little strange. Pale even."

"Too much sun," she lied.

"Too much sun? There is nothing but shade around this house right now."

"Maybe too much kissing, then," she laughed.

"I will gladly give you a little more," he offered.

"Then I would surely faint," she teased.

"I would hold on to you," he promised.

"I see you are all prepared to brave the trellis, so let's have at it."

"If you insist, slave driver," He trudged out to the trellis again, with Loraine in his wake.

"If I fall, you had better catch me," he grinned.

"Oh, sure, sure, you think I want to get killed as well?"

Lawrence grabbed onto the trellis and gave it a shake to estimate its strength. "Seems sturdy enough," he mumbled, and reached up, pulling himself up onto it, standing for a few minutes to see if it would hold his weight. Then he took another step, as he swore at the vines that were grabbing the sleeves of his jacket.

"Why did I ever agree to this?" he moaned, and took another step.

Loraine watched breathlessly, crossing her fingers that the trellis held and he did not come crashing down into her lap, because she was sure she would try to break his fall, if he did come crashing down. Finally he reached the window. He held on with one hand, while he tried to work the window with the other hand.

"No use! The window is locked. The blinds are pulled. I can't even see into the room, and short of breaking the window, there is no way to get in."

"Okay. I guess you had better come down while the trellis is still holding," Loraine suggested. "What a waste of a good kiss!"

"I can't help it if I couldn't get in. At least I tried climbing it, at the risk of immanent death, I might remind you!" He climbed down and jumped the last couple of feet, landing in front of her. "Well, that didn't work... what next?"

"I don't know."

"We can't remove the door, because the hinges are on the inside. I don't think it would be right to break the window, or force the door, so maybe that room is never going to be opened."

"I don't understand why a new key cannot be made."

"Don't think they make them anymore. If we could take the door knob off, we might be able to get it opened that way, but those old door knobs are not easy to take apart with the door still closed. And I bet the screws are on the inside anyway. The whole purpose of being able to lock a door is to make sure no one on the outside can just loosen a couple of screws and come on in."

"I guess this is going to be a project for another day," Loraine frowned. She had so hoped she could get into the room, and now it looked like they were never going to find out anything more about Loraine of the past.

"I'm going to be done working out here in another couple of hours. Then I am going back to your aunt's house and get cleaned up. You want to come out to dinner with me later?"

"Knowing my aunt, she will have a dinner planned for you, by the time you get back. You wouldn't want to disappoint her and go out to eat," Loraine pointed out.

"Okay then. Why don't you come over to your Aunt's house to eat, just to show her there are no hard feelings about her letting me have your room," he suggested.

"I don't know. I think I should let her stew a little bit longer."

"You are so cold hearted."

"Probably, but it was a mean thing for her to do, before she even found out if I had gotten the job. I would have been sleeping on the couch in the den, if I hadn't gotten hired here."

"Oh, I would have shared your bed with you," he grinned, and winked.

"I'm sure you would. Then my Aunt would have kicked you out as well."

"Since you won't come to dinner with me, how about coming out with me Saturday night? It can be a real date, and I will let your aunt know in advance that I won't be there for dinner."

"I don't know. I will be seeing you almost every day. Do we have to spend the nights together too? You might find me pretty boring."

"Boring you are not, and I wouldn't mind spending every night with you, my dear. After that kiss, it is going to take a while for my heart to start beating right again. And as far as I'm concerned, you can keep my heart skipping a beat any time."

"I'll think about it. I'll let you know Friday."

"Playing hard to get, I see."

"I *am* hard to get. I am not interested in men right now… no matter how good they kiss. If you want my company it will only be on a friendship basis, and nothing more."

"At this point, I will settle for anything," he said truthfully, feeling his heart fall a little bit, but then he was a determined person. He was not going to give up very easily. There was something about her that had pulled at him, the first moment he bumped into her at her Aunt's house. After that kiss, the feeling got even stronger. It almost felt as though he had kissed her before, she seemed so familiar to him, but for now he would have to play it cool.

Lawrence went back to work, tearing ivy off of the brick wall around the patio, because it was taking over the whole house and he wanted to get it away from the windows. There was enough ivy as it was, growing up trees, and fences, not to mention the front porch columns. Loraine went and sat down at the picnic table, to look over all the photographs of the house that Amelia had given Lawrence to look at. There were not only pictures of the outside of the house, but also of different rooms in the house. Probably the ones her grandfather had given her so she could work on the doll house, and make it look like the real rooms in the house.

Every room seemed to pull at her, as though they were

calling to her. She hadn't even seen the whole house on the inside. Only the rooms in the doll house, and yet these rooms seemed so familiar. But that was probably because she had seen them in the doll house, and she remembered them as she looked at each room. But that did not explain why the pictures of the outside of the house seemed to grab her and make her feel nostalgic.

The radio music was still blaring, and Lawrence was swearing at the ivy, which was not cooperating, and clung to the house as though it would never let go. He grabbed a thick strand, and was wrestling with it, coaxing and swearing, as he yanked against it. Suddenly the strand gave way, and Lawrence went sprawling across the patio.

Loraine dropped the pictures and ran over to him, to make sure he wasn't hurt. "Are you okay?" she asked as she knelt by his side and bent over him, looking anxiously into his face. His eyes were closed, and when he heard her voice they slowly fluttered open.

"Now I am," he grinned, as he reached up one hand and pulled her head down for a kiss. She swatted his hand away, but not until he had gotten what he wanted, and gave her a triumphant smile, which deepened the dimple in his cheek.

"That was pretty sly of you. I guess I will have to keep my distance, after this. Next time I will just let you lie there and bleed to death."

"No blood here, just a scraped elbow." He rubbed his elbow, as he jumped up to his feet again, and pulled the long strand of ivy, back away from the house. "That damn vine was clinging so tight, I thought I would never get it lose, and look, it loosened that brick." He went closer to investigate, to see how much damage it did, and if any other bricks had been loosened by the clinging vine.

The brick was sticking half way out of the wall, and Lawrence tried to push it back in, but it wouldn't go. Probably some mortar fell down behind it, he thought, and pulled the brick the rest of the way out, sticking his fingers in the hole to pull out the lose mortar. Instead of finding mortar though, he found a small box.

"Hey, Loraine, come take a look at this," he called as he took the lid off of the small wooden box. Loraine came and looked over his shoulder.

"What did you find?"

He slammed the lid back on the box. "Oh, ho, ho. You are not going to believe this!" he laughed excitedly.

"Believe what? Let me see." She grabbed for the box but he held it up over his head.

"This calls for another kiss. Not only to see what is in the box, but because what is in the box is something you want very badly!"

"The key, you found the key?"

He puckered up his mouth and pointed to it. "All you have to do is place one right here!" he instructed.

"Oh…you are infuriating!"

"You want the key or not?"

"Yes, yes, yes!" She jumped up and tried to grab the box out of his hand, but he just dodged her.

"I will gladly give it to you, for a price…."

"What is with you, always wanting to kiss me?"

"Because your lips are so delicious, and I know you will never kiss me willingly, so I have to use any ploy I can find."

"Let me see the key first. You could be lying."

He opened the box over his head and tipped it slightly so she could see inside. There was a key there.

Loraine started jumping up and down as he snapped the box closed and held it behind his back. He raised his eyebrows, and puckered his mouth again, as he stretched out his neck.

"Kissy, kissy," he demanded.

"Oh!" She stepped forward, and gave him a peck on his puckered lips, but he grabbed her and held her tight as he captured her lips beneath his mouth in a hard, demanding kiss. Loraine resisted, but Lawrence refused to loosen his hold, and eventually she started to relax, as his kiss coaxed her resistance to the surface and melted it away. She found her traitorous arms defying her, and reaching up around his neck, as he continued the kiss, gaining passion as he did so.

Finally she pulled away. "Okay, okay, you got what you wanted, now give me the key!"

"You can't tell me, you didn't enjoy that as much as I did," he demanded.

"Doesn't matter, you got it by bribing me, which seems to be your mode of operation. If not blackmailing me, or bribing me, you are just stealing kisses at every opportunity. I am going to have to keep my distance from you, after this."

"One of these days, I am not going to have to use any ploys to get you to kiss me," he predicted.

"I don't see it happening in this lifetime," she rebuffed.

"Just what life did you have in mind?" he wanted to know.

"Oh, maybe in the next."

"Do you believe in reincarnation or something?"

"I don't know, but if I do have a next life, you are going to have to wait until I have it, before you ever get another kiss from me, willingly or otherwise!"

"What a spoil sport!"

Loraine held out her hand. "Ok, hand it over. You got your stolen kiss, not to mention all the other ones you stole without much of a reward, so I deserve that key."

"You mean kissing me was not reward enough?" Lawrence

laughed. "Here you go, Princess." He bowed and handed her the key. "Don't lose it. I think it is the only one of its kind. Can I come with you, when you try it?"

"Certainly not, if I know you, you will get me trapped in that room and demand even more kisses! Go back to your ivy pulling. Besides I am not going to try this key until after the housekeeper goes to bed. If she catches me, she may take it away from me."

"Smart move."

"I don't want to tell Amelia about the key until I find out what is in the room, so don't say anything to her. I don't want her to get her hopes up. Maybe we should wait until we discover the answers about her mother, before we tell her. She may try to find a way to get upstairs herself just to see into that room, and I don't want her hurting herself."

"Imagine waiting eighty years just to see her mother's room? What a trip!"

"I have only been here two days, and I am as excited as she is," Loraine admitted. "I sure hope I find out what she needs to know about her mother, and maybe who her father was."

"As soon as you get in there, let me know what you find," Lawrence made her promise.

"Don't worry. I don't want to tell Amelia anything until I discover the whole story, so of course I will be dying to tell someone about it, and I guess you are elected."

"Good girl. If you need my help with anything, let me know. I'm going to clean up this mess and then head out to your aunt's place."

"Okay, then I will probably see you tomorrow."

"Darn tootin'! I can't wait to hear about the locked room."

"Bye, Lawrence," she said, and then reached up and gave him a slow kiss on the mouth, which took him by surprise.

Just as he started getting into the kiss, she pulled away, and smiled. "Don't say I never gave you anything without you taking it unwillingly!" She turned and headed into the house through the back door, leaving Lawrence staring after her, his fingers to his lips.

"Well, I'll be damned," he said under his breath, as a grin stretched across his face. "...not in this life time, huh?" Then he walked away whistling.

Loraine waited until the house was quiet, and she was sure everyone had gone to bed. Earlier, she had gone to her car and gotten her flashlight out of the glove compartment, and had it ready to use. It stood to reason, if that room had been locked all those years, that when the house was updated, and electricity put in, that none had been put in that room, so there wouldn't be any light in there for her to use, and she didn't know where any candles were. The flash light would have to do for now, just for her to look around, and then tomorrow, when the housekeeper was busy, she would sneak in again, and do some serious searching.

Loraine walked quietly, the few steps from her own door to the locked room, her flashlight, poised at the key hole. As she tried to silence her beating heart, she put the key in the lock and turned it. At first it didn't act like it was going to work, but after all, the door had been locked for a very long time, and was probably pretty stiff. This had to be the key. Why else would it be hidden behind that brick in the wall? She turned harder, and finally with a little echoing click, it turned and she was able to push the door open.

Loraine shined the flashlight into the room. The space was in eerie shadow and the light beam of the flashlight distorted everything, making the shadows move like disembodied ghosts. A feeling of sadness hit her, as she slowly entered the room, and closed the door behind her. The click of the door sent a chill through her, making her fear that perhaps she would end up getting locked inside. She stuffed the key in her jeans pocket, and made sure it was pushed in snuggly. Then she looked around her.

Loraine could see a bed, and a dresser, as she scanned the room. She noticed a lot of cobwebs, and wrinkled her nose. The room felt cold, even though the weather had been warm, and it was as if icy fingers were touching her body. And yet, at the same time, there was an overwhelming familiarity about the room, like she had known what it would look like inside, all along. She stood for a moment, waiting for her heart to calm, as the flashlight wavered against cobwebs, and ghostly pieces of furniture, that almost seemed alive, as the light distorted their shadows, causing them to jump out at her.

Loraine continued to shine the light around the room. The beam caught little particles of dust that floated about the room, probably being disturbed for the first time, since Amelia had been born, and her mother had died. The shade on the window was closed, like Lawrence mentioned. The room was furnished in early turn of the century furniture, but then most of the rooms in the house were. She assumed that the house furnishings had not changed much since Amelia was a girl. The whole place was like going back in time. The bed, a canopy, similar to the one in her room, was neatly made, but in the dim light she couldn't make out the color. There were bottles of perfume and a powder box on the dressing table, along with other articles, that were covered with dust. Cobwebs stretched across the mirror at the dressing table, and connected all the bottles of perfume, and other things sitting there, together. She just hoped they were not black widow spider webs, which were one of the spiders that populated California. On the dresser, which was a high dresser, reaching to her chin, was a jewelry box, and a pair of gloves were laid carelessly beside it, as though someone had just put them there and was going to put them on.

Loraine saw a candle sitting on the night stand, with a small box of matches next to it. She took one out and struck it. It actually lit, and she put it to the candle wick. A soft glow filled the space around the night stand, and gave enough light for her to make out the shapes in the room, without having to direct the flashlight on them. It was then that she noticed some picture frames leaning against the wall. They were all facing against the wall, and Loraine approached them and turned the first picture to her and shone the flash light on it.

She gasped, and almost dropped the flash light, when she looked down at the painting before her. It was of a young woman, about her own age, and what shocked her so much, was that the woman looked like her, except that she was dressed in old fashion clothes, and she knew it was not a painting of herself. Perhaps the flashlight distorted the picture and she just thought it looked like her. After all, she had been having all these strange familiar feelings about this house, so maybe she was just imagining it. She would have to take a closer look at the painting in the daylight, she decided. Why would the woman in the painting look like her? After all, she wasn't even related to Amelia, or the long dead Loraine. She turned the rest of the pictures, there were four, and each one was of the same woman at different ages, which Loraine was sure was Amelia's mother. She put the paintings back, facing the wall, and opened the closet, where she found gowns hanging. They too, were covered with dust, and cobwebs. Shoes were placed on the floor of the wardrobe. There was a trunk at the end of the bed, and when Loraine opened it, she saw there were more clothes. Apparently they had taken everything that Loraine ever owned, and placed it in that room. In the corner was a box of old dolls, and a few stuffed animals. Another box held some books, and Loraine picked one up. The pride and the prejudice, she read the title. Another was a poem book. She wondered if maybe Loraine's diary was in this box.

She opened drawers in the dresser and saw an assortment of corsets, pantalets, stockings, gloves. Another drawer held scarves, and another held shawls. Still another held night gowns. Everything smelled musty. In the night stand drawer, was writing material, a pen and a bottle of ink, with blotter and sealing wax. Only the ink had all dried out. She found hatboxes, each with a different hat in it, and a pincushion that held hat pins. This was a treasure trove of antiques of a long ago day that had not been touched for eighty years. She sat at the dressing stool and just stared at the room around her. Her heart pounded, and she suddenly wanted to escape the room. She felt stifled, and imagined herself locked in that room. It was that same fear, she felt, when she first entered, and heard the door close. She jumped up, blew out the candle, and put her hand on the knob. It opened easily, and she let out a breath of relief. Loraine took the key and locked the door again, and went back to her own room, her pounding heart, filling her ears. She began pulling cobwebs from her hair and clothes. They felt like they were clinging to her very soul. There was something about that room that frightened her, as much as it intrigued her. She was sure she would feel better about it in the morning, though.

CHAPTER SEVEN

"Did you get into the room?" Lawrence questioned, grabbing Loraine's arm, as she came out of her own room the next morning. He had come to work early, and had been waiting outside her room to pounce on her the moment she opened the door.

"Yes," she hissed. "What are you doing here, waiting outside my room?"

"I had to find out. I could barely sleep last night just thinking about it. What did you find?"

"A room… a woman's room, much like all these other rooms, except that it was covered in cobwebs and nothing had been touched for eighty years."

"I want to see it," he demanded.

"No. I just looked at it with a flashlight. I want to investigate it some more. Then, I will think about letting you in."

"Come on, I found the key for you. That should at least count for something."

Loraine stood and stared at him, trying to decide whether it was wise to let him into the room?

"Do you promise not to try and take advantage of me

anymore? No more stolen kisses? No more blackmailing me into kissing you? No more kissing at all, unless I initiate it?"

"Man, you drive a hard bargain!"

"Well?"

"You are just taking all the fun out of life!"

"I guess that means you don't want to see the room then?" Loraine started to turn away, but he grabbed her hand.

Lawrence looked down into her eyes. "You know I could never get enough of kissing you, and I want to get to know you better, but if you would rather have it on your terms and keep me at arm's length until I get you to fall madly in love with me, and you can't wait to jump my bones, then I will have to concede."

"Good. Then I won't have to worry about you trying to kiss me every time I turn around."

Lawrence rolled his eyes, and shook his head. "This is a great sacrifice, I want to let you know," he told her.

"Whatever. Is it a deal?"

"Okay, okay. Show me the room."

Loraine took the key from her Jean's pocket where she had left it from the night before, and walked over to the door. She fit the key into the lock, and turned it. That same hollow sound of the key turning, had a strange effect on her, but she tried to ignore it. Slowly, she pushed the door open, Lawrence stepped in and grabbed her hand, dragging her in with him, and then closed the door.

"Lock it, just to be on the safe side," he told her, and she obeyed. Only when the lock clicked, she had an irritable need to unlock the door, and rush from the room. She bravely stood her ground, telling herself, she was just trying to freak herself out, because there was such a mystery about the woman who had used this room so long ago, in time.

They both stood, looking around the room, as Lawrence gave a low whistle.

"Man, this place is a mess," he said under his breath, as he began walking around the room and looking at things. "How are you going to find out anything about her, just by looking at things in her room?"

"I am hoping to find a diary someplace, or letters, or something that might tell me about her."

Lawrence went to the box of books and picked one up, thumbing through it. He stopped, and started to read:

When I awoke, 'twas in the twilight bower;
Just when the light of morn, with hum of bees,
Stole through its verdurous matting of fresh trees
How sweet, and sweeter! For I heard a lyre,
And over it a sighing voice expire.
It ceased - I caught light footsteps; and anon
The fairest face that morn e'er looked upon

Pushed through a screen of roses. Starry Jove!
With tears, and smiles, and honey words she wove.
A net whose thralldom was more bliss than all
The range of flowered Elysium. Thus did fall.
The dew of her rich speech: 'Ah! Art awake?
O let me hear thee speak, for Cupid's sake!
I am so oppressed with joy! Why, I have shed
An urn of tears, as though thou wert cold dead;
And now I find thee living, I will pour
From these devoted eyes their silver store,
Until exhausted of the latest drop,
So it will pleasure thee, and force thee stop
Here, that I too may live: but if beyond
Such cool and sorrowful offerings, thou art fond
Of soothing warmth, of dalliance supreme;
If thou art ripe to take a long love dream;
If smiles, if dimples, tongues for ardor mute,
Hang in thy vision like a tempting fruit,
O let me pluck it for thee,' Thus she linked
Her charming syllables, till indistinct
Their music came to my o'er-sweetened soul;
And then she hovered over me, and stole
So near, that if no nearer it had been
This furrowed visage thou hadst never seen.

Loraine stared at him, a strange feeling hovering over her. She had heard those words before, and she was trying to remember who had read them to her? He smiled and let the book drop into the box.

"Keats." he said turning away.

But Loraine was standing stock still. She had never read Keats before, but the words seemed to sink into her, and they sounded familiar, and taunting. They appeared to tell a story, she could not quite figure out, of life and death and love, and something lost. She felt the tightness of the room. She remembered the door was locked, and started to panic, even though she held the key. She didn't want to be in that room, and yet she wanted to discover its secrets.

Lawrence turned around and looked at her. One look at her face, and he strode over to her, and put his arms around her.

"What is the matter? You look scared. Did you see a ghost or something?"

He could feel her trembling under his arms, and he held her tighter. Loraine laid her head on his shoulder. She felt the room spinning, and she wanted to steady herself.

"It…it was the poem. Something about it seemed to trigger some memory. I think I am all right now though." She lifted her head.

"You read Keats? Is that why it triggered a memory?"

"No...no. I have never read Keats, but something in the poem...I don't know. It seemed like I recognized it though."

"I think you need some air."

He slowly released her and went over and lifted the blind and unlocked the window and pulled it open.

"This room has been closed up a long time. It is stuffy in here."

"That must be it. I feel better now."

"Good." He went back over to her, and looked down into her face. "You sure? That poem made me feel strange too, sort of like I had read it to you before, or to someone before."

"It wasn't me."

"And I have never read Keats to anyone before either. The only time I read Keats was in collage when it was required reading." He placed his hand on her shoulder. "You sure you're okay?" She nodded, he was looking over her shoulder. "What are those?" he asked pointing to the paintings turned towards the wall.

She turned and looked, and stepped back, intending to stop him from going to them, but she was too late. He had stepped past her and was turning the paintings so the light from the window could fall upon their faces.

"Good heavens! Do you realize these paintings look like you?" Lawrence, stared at her, and then the paintings again.

In the light, Loraine could see that she had been right the

night before. The paintings *did* look like her.

"This is eerie! You look like the woman in this painting, and we know that it is probably a painting of Amelia's mother, Loraine, and your name is Loraine…"

"But I am not related to her, or you, or anyone, so why do I look like her?"

"Some sort of throwback. We are supposed to have doubles on earth, so perhaps we can be doubles of people in the past as well."

"That is why I feel so uncomfortable in this room. There is something about it that makes me feel uneasy. And you make me feel uneasy in the same way. I don't know why. I am attracted to you. I mean we all know you are a hunk, but my very attraction makes me feel…cautious…I guess is the only word to describe it."

"Are you going to be up for this? You want me to take over?"

"No! While I feel uneasy, I also feel like I have to find out. I have to find out why I look like that woman, and why this room makes me feel so strange. Why this whole house makes me feel strange. I have been drawn to it since the first time I ever saw it, when I was a child."

"Okay. But you don't look so good. Maybe you should come back later, after you have had more fresh air."

"Don't tell Amelia about me looking like her mother.

Don't even tell her we found the pictures, or got into the room. I want to do more digging before I let her know anything."

"You got it. Come on, let's get out of here."

Loraine unlocked the door, and they stepped out into the hall.

"You sure you are going to be all right?" he asked, as they walked down the stairs towards the kitchen.

"I think when I eat something, I will be feeling better, and then I am going to go back up there. I will call you from the window, when I do, just in case anything happens, you will know where I am. Only I will still lock the door, so no one but you will know I am in there."

"Well, what can happen? I can always climb the trellis if you don't come down. So leave the window open, okay?"

"Yeah, I will do that."

Loraine went into the kitchen to eat breakfast, and Lawrence went outside to continue working on the over grown garden. She couldn't help but feel there was something more to all of this than met the eye. She wondered why she felt so panicky when she was in that room. Rooms had never affected her before in that way, but she was determined to brave it, no matter what she felt. She would just control her fear, she decided.

When she finished eating, she went to look for Amelia. She heard the piano playing, and went to the front parlor. There, sitting at the piano was Amelia, playing a heart wrenching song. The melody touched Loraine's heart, and even though she had never heard that songs before, it seemed familiar to her as well. It was strangely starting to bring back vague memories of something she couldn't quite recall.

Amelia turned and saw her standing there. "Had so much time on my hands all my life, I learned to play the piano, but the only music I had was the stuff that was here before I was born. My grandfather was not very accommodating, and when I was raised, it was in the twenty's, and he believed all that 'jazz' as it was called, was not healthy for young minds. I was stuck with the old stuff."

"It sounded wonderful. I liked what you were playing."

"There was a lot of classical music as well, Beethoven, Mozart, all the old composers, so I learned them all."

"I love listening to you play."

"So what are you up to today?" Amelia asked.

"Uh, I am still trying to find a way into that room," she lied. "We even tried climbing the trellis, anyway Lawrence did, but the window was locked."

"Did you try getting Mary's keys?"

"Yes, and none of them fit."

"Oh." She looked disappointed.

"But don't worry. I will find a way into it yet, but for now,

I am going to do some more research at the library, so I will be out for a while. I am not sure how long."

"I hope you find out some more information. I keep wondering what happened to my mother, when she disappeared on her wedding day."

"So do I. I will see you later then," she said, and left the parlor. Loraine then went out and got in her car.

"Hey, I thought you were going to go into the room," Lawrence called, as he came up to the door of her car.

"I am, but I said I was going to the library so no one would wonder where I was, so I am going to park my car around the block and come back and sneak in the house and up to the room."

"Oh. Well good luck." He waved her off, and went back to work.

Loraine opened the door to the room for the third time, and stepped inside. She went over to the window, and gave Lawrence the thumbs up sign, and then turned back to the room. She didn't really know where to start. Should she look for the diary, and where would Loraine have hidden it, if she had one? Maybe in the top shelf of the wardrobe. She opened the door, and looked. There were some hat boxes and a photo album. She pulled the photo album down and started turning the pages. The book was filled with different photos of Loraine, from childhood, to adult hood, and as she looked into the eyes of that Loraine from the past, she tried to read her mind, but nothing came to her. She laid the book on the bed, and took down the hat boxes, but there were only hats in them.

Loraine began looking at the dresses hanging in the wardrobe. They were all so beautiful. The kind of dresses that no one ever wore any more, and she was certain they would never come back in style either. Back then Clothes were everything. There was more care taken in what a person wore and when they wore it that it seemed their whole life was planned around putting on clothes! Of course they did not have television to occupy their time, Loraine laughed to herself.

Her hand touched a silk suit bag and she pulled it out and unbuttoned it, to look inside. There, lying across the bed was the wedding dress that Loraine was supposed to wear on her wedding day that never took place. She smoothed her hand over it. It was long and lacy with appliquéd roses on the bodice. The sleeves were long, coming to a point with pearls sewn along the edge of the V point. The neck was high, but from the collar to the top of the bodice, it was all see through handmade lace. The dress had yellowed over the years it had hung there, but it still seemed in good condition, and Loraine could not help but hold it up to her, and look at herself in the mirror. What a lovely dress... a dress that any girl would love to get married in, and yet, Loraine probably never wore it. Well at least not in a church. The newspaper article said she had put it on, but then when her mother came back to the room, her daughter was gone, and later the dress was found hanging in the wardrobe, so Loraine probably only wore it for that short time she was in the room, before her mother came in to see her.

Without thinking, Loraine removed the dress the rest of the way from the suit bag, and found herself pulling her jeans off and putting the wedding dress over her head, fastening the buttons down the back, with some difficulty. It fit her as though it was made for her, and she turned, looking at herself in the ripple of the old mirror, looking a little misty through the dust that had collected there. As she turned, she started to feel dizzy, so she stopped turning, and caught her balance, by grabbing out for one of the posts of the four poster bed. She steadied herself, and looked at her reflection in the mirror again, but something was subtly different now.

Loraine's hair had been tied back with a ribbon, but now, as she looked at herself in the mirror, it was piled on top of her head. And something else was different; the mirror was no longer dusty looking. Had she imagined the dust? She reached her hand up to her hair, and saw that she was wearing an engagement ring, which she had never seen before. It was then that she noticed the room. It was not covered in cobwebs any longer, like the mirror the dust had disappeared. The box of books was no longer in the corner, nor the box of old dolls. There was no more dust on the surface of the furniture, and the room was immaculately clean. Her Jeans were not lying on the floor where she had left them. She was now wearing silk slippers, not her sandals that she had been wearing when she put the dress on.

Loraine took in her breath, but before she could think of what to do, there was a knock on the door. She wondered if Mary Mathews had discovered she was in the room and was going to root her out. Before she could even respond to the thought, the door was pushed open, and a woman that Loraine had never seen before in her life, came into the room and smiled at her.

"Are you almost ready dear?" the woman asked, as she took in Loraine with tender grey eyes.

Loraine realized that this was her mother. The thought just came to her, and she knew that she was about to be married, and this was her mother coming in to check on her.

It couldn't be! Was she transported back in time? This was the day that Amelia's mother was going to get married, and she seemed to be the Loraine of the past. She could feel it. She didn't want to get married. It was a revulsion that she felt in the very pit of her stomach. Then the thought of 'him' came into her mind. She was in love with 'him'. At the moment she wasn't quite sure who 'him' was, but she knew she loved someone else, and did not want to get married to Gaston.

Her mother smiled. "Hurry down. Everyone is waiting. You don't want to be late." She went out and closed the door.

Loraine felt a sudden panic. There was no way she was going to marry that man! She would go find 'him'. The man she loved, and run away with him! She turned back to her wardrobe, and pulled out a yellow muslin dress. She started tearing at the buttons of the wedding dress, and ripping it from her body, as her heart pounded. The beautiful dress fell in a puddle around her feet, and then Loraine's head started to clear. The room turned back to the cobweb filled room again, but the yellow dress was still lying on the bed where she had placed it. Her jeans were now on the floor beside the wedding dress.

Loraine sank down onto the bed, her heart pounding hard. What had happened? She was sure she had been back in the past. Had Loraine's mother of the past really come into the room? Was it all in her head? But there was the yellow dress laying there, and she had not put it there until after she had put on the wedding dress and been transported back in time.

Loraine sat staring at the yellow dress. What would happen if she put it on, she wondered? With shaking fingers she picked it up. Then she stood up, and slipped it over her head. Once again the room changed. The wedding dress was still in a pile at her feet. She picked it up and put it neatly into the suit bag and hung it in the wardrobe. Then she turned to the window. She was going to go out the window and climb down the trellis!

No! She couldn't do that! If she went outside, she may get trapped in time, and not be able to come back to the room and find herself again. She didn't know what would happen if she left the house? One part of her was rushing to the window, and the other part of her, was trying to hold herself back. She lifted the window and looked out. Everything was so different than it had been when Lawrence was working on the yard. It was all neat and trimmed, and the roses had not grown to the top of the trellis yet. With great effort, she pulled away from the window, and started to take the dress off again. As she did so, the room once again changed, and she found herself back in her own time.

She was breathing hard. Her heart was racing! She had actually become Loraine of the past, when she put on those old clothes! This was amazing! She wondered if it would always happen if she put on Loraine's clothes of the past. But for now, she had enough blinking into the past. It frightened her, even though it also intrigued her as well. This was very, very peculiar, and she did not know what to make of it.

Trying to slow the beating of her heart, Loraine gulped in more air, and finished getting dressed back into her jeans. She now realized that this would be a way to discover more about Loraine of the past. Somehow she was connected to this woman, or at least when she was wearing the woman's clothes, she was connected to her. But it must be more than that, she reasoned, because from the very beginning, she had been trying to ignore all the things that drew her to the house, and the familiarity of it all. She remembered how she still felt when she was in this locked room, and how uneasy it made her. There was something here that she needed to discover, more than just why Loraine did not marry, or want to marry the banker. She felt she needed more answers than just discovering who Amelia's father had been. Even though she was not related to Amelia, she felt she had a deep connection to her, and she wanted to discover that connection as well.

She wondered if she should confide in Lawrence or not? Would he even believe her, she wondered? If she could be transported back in time, every time she put on one of Loraine's dresses, she may be able to unravel all of this, but someone had to know about it, in case she got trapped in the past. She may just disappear some day and no one would ever know what happened to her.

She thought about the revulsion she had felt about marrying Gaston, and wanted to find out more about the banker. She wanted to find out why the shoe company had gone out of business, and what connection it all had to Loraine marrying the banker? For some reason her parents were forcing her to marry the banker, and she was in love with someone else. Even though marriages were sometimes arranged back then, she knew from the very depth of her soul that Loraine hated the banker, and would rather run away than get married to him.

She left the room, and relocked the door, then placed the key back in her pocket. Trying to steady herself, she walked down the stairs, and headed out to the garden. She was amazed when she saw how much work Lawrence had gotten done on it. It was really starting to shape up, and begin to look like the pictures she had looked at the day before. She could hear the music and followed the sound until she located where Lawrence was working. He had cleared some of the paths that lead through the back garden, now that he had removed all the ivy from the back of the house, and had trimmed it back from the trees, and fences.

He was now working around a dried up fish pond that had benches placed around it, only up until then the benches had been lost in the over growth, and the pond itself had been over grown with plants that came up from the cracks in the cement. Loraine sat down on one of the benches and watches as he pulled plants and weeds out of the pond. He suddenly seemed to notice her, and climbed up out of the pond, and sat down beside her.

"Well, Nancy Drew, have you found anything interesting?"

Loraine was quite. She still wasn't sure if she should tell Lawrence anything. He would think her crazy, or having a nervous-breakdown or something, if she told him what really happened.

"Hey, that bad huh? Didn't you even find the diary?"

"No, I didn't find the diary. But I found the wedding dress."

"The wedding dress she never wore to her wedding. That must have been sad."

"She didn't want to marry the man. She hated him. She was in love with someone else!"

"I thought you said you didn't find the diary. What did you find, love letters or something?"

"No...I...I found the wedding dress, so I decided to try it on. Once I had it on, I knew just what she was thinking when she wore it."

"Don't tell me you are physic!"

"Maybe I am. Maybe that is why it all happened."

"Why what all happened?"

"Knowing what she was thinking, and sort of going back in time, while I had that dress on."

"This is interesting. So what happened?"

"Oh, you won't believe me, even if I told you."

"Why don't you try me?"

"And then be ridiculed by you?"

"I would never do that. I like you."

Loraine took a deep breath, and studied Lawrence's face. He had a smudge of dirt on his face, and she reached up with her hand, and brushed it away. Her hand on his cheek felt good, and he wished she had left her hand there a little longer. He wanted to grab her hand and hold it, but he had promised her not to make any more passes at her. He could not forget though, how he had felt when he was kissing her, and now that part of their relationship may never be rekindled again. She was being so cold and distant. Even talking to him now seemed to take some effort on her part, he thought. She was being careful about what she was saying. He could feel it. She didn't trust him, but how could he blame her? He had been hitting on her from the moment he met her.

"You know what I'm thinking?" she said almost to herself. "There must be some sort of records of the business. Somehow the Banker is linked to all of this. The business was going under, according to Amelia, by the time she was born they had lost the business. A bank makes loans to businesses. Maybe that is why they wanted Loraine to marry the banker, to help shore up the business. What better way, than to have a banker become part of the family? Then when Loraine didn't marry the banker everything went kaput!"

"Maybe Amelia knows where the records are kept. If we could get a look at them, we could find out why the business failed. Amelia said there was a fire, but insurance should have covered that, unless there wasn't any insurance, and no halfway decent business man would fail to insure his company in case of loss or fire."

"You're right. Let's go ask Amelia, and then would you help me go through the files?"

"Sure. I need a rest from all this physical labor," he laughed, "And besides you would make much better company than these weeds and over grown plants."

They stood up from the bench and headed back into the house.

"I think it is getting close to lunch time, anyway," Loraine said. "We can ask Amelia about it while we eat lunch. By the way, how was Aunt Mel's dinner last night?"

"Pot roast, the best!"

"She is a good cook."

"Your cousin was asking about you, and how it was working out for you here. I told him you were in your element."

"Later, we should tell him all about what we have been finding. He likes a good mystery."

"Yeah, maybe you and I and he and his girlfriend…does he have one?…, should all get together and do something as a group."

"No steady girlfriend, but he is so good looking, it isn't hard for him to find a date."

"Why don't I invite him out with us Saturday night then?"

"I never said if I was going out with you Saturday," she reminded him.

"Oh, you know you're coming, so I will ask him."

"Don't be taking me for granted, you may end up being put in your place."

"Okay, are you coming or not?"

"I suppose I could make it, as long as my kissing cousin is there to protect me."

"Maybe I will have to protect you from *him*. He is constantly talking about you. I think he is as much in love with you as I am."

Loraine ignored his statement about his love for her, and pretended like she hadn't heard it. "He better not be telling you things about me, that stinker!"

"Too late, he and I have long conversations about you. In another day or so, I will know all there is to know about you!"

"I think I need to give my cousin a talking to!" Loraine complained, and then catching sight of Amelia, said, "There's Amelia going into the kitchen now. Let's go catch up with her."

They both headed for the kitchen. Loraine was glad for the interruption in the conversation, since she didn't want to hear how either he or her cousin felt about her. She remembered how disappointed she was that Randy was her cousin, when she discovered she had such strong feelings for him, and of course Aunt Mel was not going to put up with any close relationship between them, and made it very clear, when she caught Randy kissing her, even though it was an innocent kiss at the time.

Strange that he was the only man who had caused any passionate feelings to grow in her, after all the years of feeling nervous any time she got close to men? It was so unexpected. But then, she remembered how she felt when Lawrence made her kiss him, and her face started to feel warm. She would never let him know how much that kiss had shaken her resolve of noninvolvement with men. Especially noninvolvement with him!

CHAPTER EIGHT

When Lawrence and Loraine approached Amelia, and explained how they wanted to look through her Grandfather's records of the shoe company business, she called Mary Mathews and asked her for the key to her grandfather's office. The office had been closed after her grandfather had died, and was only opened once a month when it needed dusting and vacuuming. It was none of Mary's concern if they wanted to go through old records, and she happily handed over the key. She was surprised they were not demanding the key to the locked room. But then, of course, she didn't even have that key, only she didn't think that anyone knew it. She knew how obsessed Amelia was with that room though.

After they had eaten, Loraine and Lawrence headed to the office. He opened the door, and Loraine went in ahead of him. The room was dim because the drapes were all pulled shut, and Lawrence walked over to the windows and pushed the drapes back, allowing the bright sunshine to filter in through the vines, that Lawrence had not yet gotten to at the front of the house, since the office faced out to the front.

Loraine had walked over to the desk, but gave an

exasperated noise when she discovered the drawers were locked, and so was the filing cabinet.

"There must be a key to the desk. I wonder if Mary has it?"

"If she had the key, she would have offered it when she gave us the key to the room. She knew we were going to look through the files."

"Then the key must be in here somewhere. Where would you hide the key?"

"Start looking in the cubby holes of the desk top," he suggested.

Loraine put her fingers into each cubby hole, with no luck. There were some small books propped up against the side of the desk, under the cubby holes, and when she pulled her hand away, she accidentally knocked them over. As they fell, one fell open and Loraine exclaimed with joy, when she discovered that the book that had fallen open was a hollow book, and there, inside, was a small bunch of keys.

"How unique," Lawrence drawled, when she showed him the book of keys. "Let's start trying them."

Loraine took the keys and tried each one in the main drawer, which she knew would unlock the rest of the drawers, once it was open. When they found the one that worked there, Lawrence started trying the other keys in the filling cabinet, while

Loraine pulled out the drawers of the desk and started investigating them.

The main drawer just held pens and personal writing paper, ink, old stamps, envelopes, paper clips, a stapler, and other odds and ends. She pulled out the top drawer on the left, and found unused receipt books, bottles of glue, more envelopes, and a large ream of paper with the company heading on it. Ledgers, but not one pertaining to the shoe business, they all had to do with the expenses of running the house, and paying the servants. Next to the ledgers was a box of unused typewriter ribbon. She opened the top drawer on the right, and found a bundle of old bills... telephone, electricity, heating fuel, repairs done on the house. A couple of old calendars, which had not been thrown away, lay under the stack of bills, which Loraine found was interesting because they dated back to the second world war. She picked the calendars up to examine them, and saw under them was a pile of newspaper clippings. The first one she recognized right away as the announcement of Loraine's engagement, and then the one about her disappearance on her wedding day, and the next one about her being found, but no comment was given. The last one, Loraine almost dropped. She held it with trembling hands.

"Lawrence, look at this!"

Lawrence stopped what he was doing and came to Loraine's side.

"This is terrible! I don't think we should tell Amelia!"

"I thought Loraine died giving birth to Amelia. It never occurred to me that she had committed suicide! No wonder they locked her room. But why would she do it, and leave her new born baby to be raised by the father who tried to force her to marry Gaston, and keep her from her true love? It must have been because Amelia was illegitimate and she couldn't face the fact."

"Boy, this sucks! Looks like we are turning up things that no one really wants to know about."

"I don't think I would want to know if my mother committed suicide. Especially, right after I was born. It would make me feel like my mother did not love me enough to stay and raise me. No wonder, I hate that locked room. They found her hanging out of the window. She had tied one of her sashes from a robe to the leg of a table placed by the window, tied it around her neck, and then climbed out on the trellis and jumped. I guess she did not try jumping out of the window to kill herself because she was afraid the fall may not kill her, and may just cripple her or something."

"Poor woman, she was so beautiful too," Lawrence commented, as he looked at the picture they had put of her in the newspaper article with the story. "It's like looking into your face though, Loraine."

Loraine started to replace the clippings, but then laid them on the desk as she reached farther back in the drawer. When she saw the note, she knew exactly what it was. Her fingers shook as she opened it.

Father, (I hesitate to call you that!)

By the time you find this note, you will have also found me dead. I am leaving my poor daughter behind for you to raise. She will remind you, until your dying day, why I killed myself. She will make you repent of ever keeping secrets from your family, and causing them to believe a falsehood. The one happiness I could have had in life, you have robbed me of, and there is no way to find any more happiness in this world, not even through my own daughter, because, eventually, I will have to tell her the truth, which will have to be covered up until she is an adult, because of your own lies. She will always want to know who her father is, and I cannot face the questions I know she will ask. You have not only tried to manipulate my life to your own purposes, but you also manipulated others before me, and now you have brought a curse upon your own head. How exacting the price when we try to save someone from the truth, we only create a hell for them. I hope you will be more honest with my daughter, than you ever were with me, until you were forced to tell me the truth.

Loraine

Loraine let the note drop to the desk, which Lawrence

picked up and started to read. Something deep within Loraine started to well up inside. She felt the pain of the woman who had written the note. She felt the anguish, and lost hope. The hatred for her life, and what her father had done to her life, and her heart reached out to her, beyond the grave, but it seemed like she was reaching out to herself, trying to comfort her own grief, though she did not know what the grief was, except for her great sadness that Amelia's mother had to die in this manner, and that Amelia's own grandfather had something to do with it.

She did not realize that she was crying, until she felt Lawrence's arms go around her and pull her up to him, bringing her to a small leather couch, and pulling her down beside him, as he cradled her in his arms.

"It's okay. It's okay." he kept telling her. "It happened a long time ago. You didn't even know the woman."

"I...I...didn't tell you what happened to me in the locked room," she sniffed, trying to control her tears. "Somehow I am connected to that woman. I can feel her pain as surely as though it was my pain," she confessed.

"What happened in the locked room?" Lawrence demanded, as he stroked her hair and held her close against his shoulder.

She pulled back and looked at him through her misty green eyes, and his dark eyes seemed to be penetrating her soul. Then she laid her head back on his shoulder, as she spoke. "Remember I told you when I put the wedding dress on, I could feel her thoughts?"

"Yes, I thought you were psychic."

"Well it wasn't just that. I not only could feel her thoughts, but the whole room changed before my eyes. I was actually transported back in time. The room was new and clean, and her mother, my mother, came into the room to see if I was ready yet, but when she went out, I knew I didn't, I mean that Loraine of the past knew she didn't want to marry Gaston. I hated the man...she hated the man! I had...she had a lover that she wanted to go to. But it was me. The emotions were mine, not hers. We shared the emotions. I knew I was Loraine of today, but I also knew I was Loraine of the past as well. I wanted to run away, so I put out a dress on the bed, in order to change out of the wedding dress, but when I took the gown off, I was back in the cobweb room again! You can't imagine how I felt! I was frightened, but at the same time I wanted to know what happened, so I put the dress on, that I had put out on the bed, and there I was, back in time again. I was going to climb out of the window so I could run off with my lover. You don't know how hard it was for me to keep myself from climbing out that window and going down the trellis, but I was afraid if I left the room I would get trapped in time or something, so I forced myself to take the dress off. I think that if I put on another dress of hers, I will experience whatever she was doing at the time she wore the dress."

Lawrence was very quiet. It scared Loraine because he was so quiet and did not say anything. He just kept patting her back, and stroking her hair. Then finally, at last, he said in a very quiet voice, "You know, I was watching you walk down the stairs ahead of me the other day, and I could have sworn you were dressed in a gown of that era. I had to do a double take, before you changed back again, and that was before you ever tried on the wedding dress."

"Then you feel it too?"

"I don't know. I feel something strange. I am not quite sure what it is?"

"The next time I go to that room, I want you to come with me, and see what happens to me, when I put on one of her dresses."

"I don't know if I am up to that..."

"You have to. I am afraid I might not come back to my own time period, and if you are there, at least you will know where I disappeared to."

Lawrence held her away from him and looked down into her eyes, which had stopped spilling tears. "Are you sure you are up to doing that? What if you do disappear into time?"

"If I do, then maybe I could change the past, and stop

Loraine from committing suicide."

"Do you really think anyone can change the past?"

"I stopped myself from going out that window to meet my lover, didn't I? I can feel both her and myself when I am in her clothes, so I have some control over the situation."

"But just because you did not go out the window, does not mean that she did not go out the window, the minute you took that dress off again. I guess you are right to have me come with you, though. I don't want you going into the past without me being there, as scary as it sounds to me. I just don't want to lose you. If you ended up going back to the past and staying, I would have to find some way to follow you there."

He looked so serious and frightened, that Loraine realized that he did have some sort of feeling for her, beyond physical attraction, and wanting to trick her into kissing him all the time. There was something in his eyes that went beyond the regular flirting of the opposite sex.

"Don't worry, I'll find a way back, so I can tell Amelia what really happened concerning her mother. But we can't say anything to her about any of this, until we discover the answers ourselves."

"I agree. There is nothing I wouldn't do to keep from hurting that old woman. So far her life has been lonely and miserable, and now she is going to discover things about her past that will make it even worse. I hate her bastard of a Grandfather, for what he did, whatever it was. That is what I want to find out."

"Yes, me too, but I also want to find out what Gaston has to do with all of this mess. I get the feeling, from Loraine of the past, that he has some sort of pull on her father, like he was holding something over his head to get him to force Loraine to marry him. I just don't know what it was. We need to find those business files, and see if they might lead us to the answers."

"You're right. I found the keys that fit the file drawers, so I guess we can start there. I'll take the top drawer, and you can take the next drawer, until we find something that might give us some answers."

For about a half hour the room was silent of voices. Only the rustle of paper filled the air, as each was lost in their search of the files in order to discover why the company failed.

"Everything seemed to be going great, until the fire," Lawrence commented.

"You have the early files. According to these, Loraine's grandfather had to borrow more money from the bank, because the insurance money did not cover all the loss. But there shouldn't have been any problem. He put the house up as collateral, and got everything up and running again."

"I'll check the bottom drawer and see what those files say." Lawrence opened the bottom drawer, as Loraine continued to look at the files she had in her hand.

"Hey, I think I discovered the problem," Lawrence exclaimed. "They were doing well on making new product, but the orders kept getting lost. It seems like they got complaints that nothing showed up. They would send out new orders, while they hunted for the lost orders, and they would not show up either. They started running out of capital to make more product, and had to borrow more from the bank to do it. The old man had to cash in some stocks to cover his losses, but didn't have enough money to fill up the orders again. Then he stopped getting orders because no one could rely on the merchandise getting there. He hired some investigators, but they came up empty handed, and he couldn't afford to hire more. Okay, this looks like it was happening right around the time Loraine was planning to get married to the banker. The very man who ran the bank that furnished the loans, I might add."

"I knew the banker had something to do with all of this, but why was he so set on marrying Loraine? I can see if he had, it would have helped her father out of a tight spot, but Loraine seemed reluctant."

"Yes, but the banker may have been over extending himself as well. If he kept bailing Loraine's father out, the bank would start losing money as well. Considering that the orders kept getting lost, which is highly unlikely, considering that before the fire, the orders made it out just fine, I think something fishy was going on."

"But who was causing it?"

"According to my sources, the New York Landons, sent Lawrence out to find out why that branch of the business was failing. You would think they had money to do some investigating. Even though the companies were run by different brothers, at different ends of the U.S., it was still a combined family business. The failure of one branch could create problems for the other branch, since they both used the family name. And back in those days, the family name was everything, and business deals could make or break a family business, no matter how many miles apart they were."

"But Loraine's father claimed that Lawrence left shortly after his sister did."

"That is what you are going to have to find out, if you are able to get back into the past again. If Lawrence did leave, then what happened to him? Once we find that out, then we will know if there was some foul play going on."

"All right, but I think I have had enough of sleuthing for one day. My head is starting to hurt, and all the things we have found out are upsetting me."

Lawrence started putting files back into the drawers, and then they locked everything up.

"I'm going to ask Randy to come out with us Saturday, when I get back, so he will have time to find a date," Lawrence told her.

"Okay. I think I am actually looking forward to going out, just in order to get out of this house for a while. It is starting to affect me."

"I know what you mean. I keep getting strange vibes as I work in the garden, and now you are starting to melt into the past of this house, which I am sure can be pretty scary."

"Only, it just happens when I put on Loraine's clothes. Anyway I hope that is the only time it will happen. I have had a couple of unsettling memories, and flashbacks of being here in the past, even before I put on the dress."

"Just be careful, Loraine. I don't want anything to happen to you, and whatever you do, if you come up at the time of Loraine's suicide, get out of that room! Rip your clothes off if you have to, but whatever you do, don't follow through with what she did back then."

"No, no I won't. I stopped myself from climbing out that window, and she really wanted to go out that window and down the trellis, so I think I have control of some of my actions independent of her."

"I sure hope so. But just because you won't do something when you are visiting the past, it doesn't mean the incident never happened anyway. It probably goes on just as before on some other level you are not aware of. This is turning out to be more than either of us expected, I'm afraid." He put his arms around her again and held her close to him. "Just take care of yourself, is all I ask," he whispered against her hair, and it felt good to have him holding her like that, she thought.

CHPATER NINE

"These earrings look good with this dress," Loraine thought, as she peered at herself in the mirror over the dressing table. She loved the yellow room, but felt drawn to the pink room, which was the color of the locked room. Loraine had decided to clean up the pink room, since she planned to spend some time in there, so-called time traveling, if she could, but she was going to leave the time traveling until next week, to give herself a break from dwelling in the past so much.

She couldn't use the vacuum in there, because the housekeeper would hear it and come investigate, and there were no outlets in there anyway, but she took a duster and broom, and cleaned all the cobwebs out, and shook the spread of the bed out the window, and wiped down all the tables and dressers with a damp cloth. The wall paper in the pink room was just like the wallpaper in the yellow room, but it was pink instead. The bedspread was the same as well, except it had pink rose buds on it. In Fact the pink room was almost a twin to the yellow room, except for the color, and some of the furniture was different.

Loraine drew her mind back to her reflection. Her hair was so long, she was always at a loss as to what she should do with it, when she didn't just wear it down her back, or pulled back and tied in a long tail. Sometimes she braided it, to keep it out of her face, but tonight she twisted it into an oblong bun and pinned it to the back of her head, letting a few stray strands wisp about her face. The dress she wore was green, and matched her eyes and earrings exactly.

She applied dark mascara to her long thick lashes, and put liner on her lower lid, which made her eyes look so much larger, and even a little innocent. She didn't like dark lipstick, so she applied light pink that had a little sparkle in it to make her lips appear moist. The dress was strapless, and though it was simple, it was long and reached to her ankles. It was a light material that the breeze caught easily and ruffled about her ankles.

With her hair up, her tan stood out all the more, and her shapely shoulders were more pronounced by the strapless dress. She sprayed a dash of C'est la Vie, an old perfume she had gotten for her birthday, which was hard to find, over her bare shoulders, and then put on a single string of fake pearls.

The sash of the dress was white, and contrasted against the green, as it fell against the long skirt, down the back, just as the pearls contrasted against her dark tan. White Grecian sandals encased her small feet, and the pink painted toenails matched her lipstick. She didn't wear any pantyhose, because she felt it was too hot in the early summer to put them on, so she could feel the breeze against her legs, as it billowed her skirt when she started down the steps to where Lawrence had parked his car in front.

When she opened the door to Lawrence's ring, before Mary could get to it, he let out a low whistle while he took in her beauty, and her bare shoulders. He could smell that same perfume she always wore, which he couldn't quite place with any other perfume he had smelled in the past.

Amelia had wheeled into the entry, and she was beaming at the two young people. "I am so happy to see you two getting along so well," she said as she came up to the door to greet Lawrence. "It has been so nice to have both of you here. You have filled the house with laughter, and excitement. The grounds are starting to look like they did when I was a young girl, and the gloom seems to have left the house. I am so glad both of you have come here."

"We are happy to be here," Lawrence assured her. "I have really enjoyed working on taming the jungle of your garden, and we are making a little headway on discovering things about your mother. When you have some time, we can tell you some of the things that we found."

"I have nothing but time," she smiled up at him. "I am getting older though, so I don't know how many more years I have for this life, but as long as I am alive, I have all the time in the world."

Loraine patted her hand. "Next week we'll tell you about the business files we found. I know it was all before you were born, but it might shed some light on why your mother was supposed to marry the banker. Only we have to do a little more investigating before we can come up with the answer. The things in the office were just what we needed to get a few answers. But you know one answer always leads to more questions that need to be answered as well."

"Yes, I am sure you are right, dear. I suppose I could have done my own investigating, but you know, I didn't have the heart. I was almost afraid of what I would find. Yet, at this stage of my life, it really doesn't matter what I find. I am not much longer for this world anyway, so what difference would it make?"

"I just hope we can help you find the answers you need to know, so you can die peacefully, knowing about your mother, and possibly who your father was."

"Yes, it would be nice to know who my father was, even though nothing can be done about it at this late date."

"Except that you would know," Lawrence offered.

"Yes…I would know. And I hope to find out why my grandfather wanted to forget that my mother ever existed. He never mentioned her name, as I told you, and even my middle name was never used. Something must have been very painful to him to cause that."

Loraine and Lawrence looked at each other knowingly, and nodded. "Well, we need to get going. Randy and his very good looking date, is waiting for us. We are all going to meet at the Bali Hi, in San Diego. Randy says it is a great place to eat. Lawrence smiled.

"And expensive," Loraine added.

"I told you I was independently wealthy," he grinned.

"Oh, yeah, I forgot. After seeing you sweat and get all dirty, I thought you were one of us."

He laughed, and the dimple showed in his cheek. Loraine reached up and touched it. "You have the cutest dimple..."

He took her hand from his face, and led her out the door, waving back at Amelia, and then closed it behind them.

"And you have the cutest fingers," he whispered, as he lifted her hand to his lips and kissed the tips of her fingers, that had just touched his dimple. He then tucked her hand under his elbow as he walked down the steps with her to his car. "And what is that smell you keep wearing? I have never smelled it before."

"It is called C'est la Vie. A very old French perfume which is quite hard to find any longer. It has to be ordered special. It was the last thing my father gave me, before he died. The name means, Such Is Life."

"I love how it smells on you," he whispered against her ear, as he drew in a deep breath.

She merely smiled, and he held the door open for her to climb into his car. He got in himself on the driver's side, depressed the clutch, started the motor, shifted gears, and then sped off in the direction of Shelter Island.

Randy and a cute little redhead, was waiting for them in the lobby of the Bali Hi, and Loraine could not help but size up the girl that was hanging on her cousin's arm. She laughed too much, Loraine thought, and she kept batting her eyes up at Randy like an inexperienced flirt. She wore a mini skirt, which was the first thing that turned Loraine off, yet she noticed how Lawrence looked at her long legs with some admiration. What was it with men and women's legs, she wondered? A leg was just a leg, for Christ's sake! She could almost understand their fascination with breasts, but legs just went over her head in making any sense. She wore spiked heels, which brought her almost up to Randy's nose. Randy was actually taller than Lawrence, but not by many inches. He was long and lanky, with sandy brown hair and blue eyes, while Lawrence was tall and buff with dark features. They were so different, that Loraine wondered why she was drawn to both of the men so much, She certainly did not like the girl Randy had chosen to take out.

"Hi, you guys. This is Sandra," he nodded to the mini clad bare lagged girl. "And this is my cousin, Loraine, and Lawrence, my mother's boarder."

"Nice to meet you," Sandra giggled, and offered a limp hand shake.

Loraine realized Sandra was a little nervous, but that did not change her attitude about the girl. The way she clung to Randy was almost shameless, and who would dare to wear a skirt that short and then put on red high heels, of all stupid colors?

They went to the desk and gave their names for their reserved tables, and shortly a waiter came and escorted them to the small round table in the corner, laid down menus and turned away, while the men helped the women get seated.

"Okay, the object of this pace is that they don't serve you separately. Everyone gives a different order, and they bring you an empty plate. Then they place all the dishes, that have been ordered, on the table, and we all share what has been ordered. That way we each get to taste a little bit of everything they offer, but still get our favorite dish, along with it," Randy explained.

Sandra gave a little squeal, which Loraine thought was tasteless, and Lawrence smiled, because he knew that Loraine was feeling jealous towards Randy's date. Randy liked Lawrence, so he didn't seem to mind that Lawrence was dating his cousin.

"I think I will have the Mandarin Duck," Loraine said, looking over the dishes.

"I'll take the Almond Pheasant," Lawrence added.

"Then I think I am going to order the Sweet and Sour

Prawns," Randy offered.

"Oh, I can't make up my mind between the Sesame seed Chicken, and the Sweet and sour pork,"

"Order them both," Lawrence suggested. "We are all going to share anyway."

She glanced at Randy under her lids, "But everything is so expensive here," she whispered under her breath, "It would cost a fortune, and we haven't even decided on our drinks yet."

Lawrence chuckled. "If we couldn't afford the bill, young lady, we wouldn't have brought you here, now would we?"

The pleased look that spread over Sandra's face almost embarrassed Loraine. Now she was batting her eyelashes at Lawrence, instead of Randy. What a minx, Loraine thought. Lawrence merely smiled, exposing that gorgeous dimple, and Loraine tried to keep her temper from flaring. Then she realized that she was not only feeling jealous about her cousin Randy, but she was feeling jealous of how Sandra was acting towards Lawrence as well. What had come over her, she wondered?

"So how is the sleuthing going?" Randy asked, as they waited for their meal to be served.

Loraine wanted to tell Randy all about it, but she did not want to do it in front of Sandra. She felt it was all too personal to talk about with a stranger present.

"Oh, everything is going fine," she said, trying to signal

with her eyes that she didn't want to talk about it there.

"Sleuthing?" Sandra questioned. "What's sleuthing?"

Loraine tried not to laugh, and put her hand over her mouth to stop the laughter from coming. The stupid girl didn't even know what sleuthing was!

"You have never read Nancy Drew?" Loraine questioned, trying to keep her voice calm.

"Sure, but what does that have to do with sleuthing?"

"Nothing at all!" Loraine said, as she winked at Randy.

"Sleuthing is detective work," Lawrence said kindly. "Loraine has always wanted to be a detective."

"Really?" Sandra questioned with wide innocent looking eyes. "Whatever for?"

"Oh, just for the heck of it." Loraine smiled. "You know, all those detective shows on TV, Hawaii five O, Colombo, Mc Giver, who can blow the world up with a tube of toothpaste, just tickles my imagination."

They were interrupted by the waiter bringing their drinks, served in tall glasses which were decorated by little paper umbrellas stuck in chunks of pineapples, bananas and cherries, floating at the top of the glass.

"Oh, how exciting!" Sandra gushed.

"Yes, very," Loraine added under her breath. It *was* nice, and exciting, but Sandra was making such a show of it, that

Loraine did not know how much more she could endure, and she wondered that her smart, handsome, cousin would choose such a ditz to go out with?

"I understand you have almost tamed the Jungle," Randy said to Lawrence.

"Jungle? What Jungle?" Sandra asked. "Are you from Africa, or something?" She looked questioningly at Lawrence.

Lawrence chuckled, and Loraine just shrugged and rolled her eyes. "Randy was referring to the place where I work. The Garden is like a jungle and I am trying to put it all back in order."

"Oh," Sandra said, and continued to stare at him with wide eyes.

"The Garden is coming along nicely. I have almost finished with the back, and will be working on the front real soon."

"Then he will have to start on the repair of the house, not only on the outside, but later on the inside," Loraine added. "That place will take you the rest of your life to finish, and Amelia will be dead before you are ever done."

"Oh, I am sure she has a few more years in her," Lawrence predicted.

"Do you think she will leave you the place when she dies? You, after all, are her only living relative, that any one knows about, anyway."

"I don't know. I have not talked to her about it. She can

do what she likes."

Sandra was looking from one to the other, feeling lost by the conversation, since she did not know what they were talking about, but then the food came, so they busied themselves passing around the dishes and taking a sample from each plate.

"This is the best stuff I have ever eaten in my whole life," Sandra announced, after taking a large mouth full from her plate, having trouble with the chopsticks and deciding to use her fork instead.

Loraine knew how to use chopsticks, and she noted that both Lawrence and Randy did too.

Sandra watched in amazement, as the three began eating with the chopsticks. "I don't know how you manage those things!" she admired. "I am all thumbs when it comes to chopsticks."

"Here, let me show you," Randy offered as he placed the sticks in one of Sandra's hands and tried to demonstrate to her the proper way to hold them. His head bent over hers as he leaned in to hold her hand on the sticks, and Loraine noticed how he looked down at the mounds of her breast that were probably held up by a push up bra, Loraine was sure, above the low cut neckline of her blouse.

Lawrence cleared his throat, as he too watched Randy, and then glanced at Loraine. His smile broadened. She looked at him and glared, when she saw the amusement on his face.

She leaned into Lawrence and whispered, "I have never seen anyone dressed so indecent in a place like this!"

"But this is a South Seas restaurant," he quipped, "The women didn't even wear tops on the islands back in the day..."

"Shut up! All men can think about, when they see a woman is her boobs and her hips!"

"Most important parts of the body," he teased.

Somehow, Loraine got through the meal, and tried to ignore Sandra's ditzy personality, and Randy's constant admiration of her well-shaped body. The two couples parted at the restaurant, and got into their separate cars.

"Well we know what Randy and that ditz are going to do tonight," Loraine said as Lawrence started driving away.

"What makes you think so? Just because a man admires the way a woman looks, does not mean he is going to try and jump her bones!"

"He was drooling all over her!" she exclaimed.

"So? He has the right to do that. He is single, after all, and a man."

"Yes, I see your minds seem to drift in the same direction," Loraine accused.

"Why do you begrudge him a little fun?" Lawrence wanted to know. "If he likes the girl, and she wants to jump in bed with him, what is it to you anyway?"

Loraine just looked at him. She didn't' want to answer that question. And he was silent for a while.

"Where are you going? This is not the way back to La Jolla."

"I thought we would drive out to Sunset Cliffs, and watch the waves crashing against the rocks."

Loraine loved Sunset Cliffs. There was so much power in the ocean the way it crashed against the rocks, sometimes sending spray high up over the cliffs and causing the sight seers to get drenched. Even though it was late, there was a full moon, and it shown its mesmerizing glow over the ocean, as they pulled up to Sunset Cliffs and got out of the car. Lawrence reached into the backseat and pulled out a blanket. She followed him down to the beach, not far from the cliffs. The best view was from the top of the cliffs, but at this angle on the beach, you could still see the waves crashing against the rocks and hear the roar of the water as it slammed against the cliff.

Lawrence spread the blanket out, and took a seat. Loraine lowered herself on the blanket, and he pulled her up against him, so she could use him as a back rest, while they watched the waves come crashing on the rocks in the moonlight, as they sat silently there. Lawrence placed his arms around Loraine's shoulders, sheltering them from the cool ocean breeze, as she leaned back against his chest, with her arms resting on his pulled up knees.

"When I was around thirteen, my girlfriend and I decided to join a group of other teens that were all coming out here to go grunion hunting," Loraine told him.

"Grunion hunting? What is that?" Lawrence questioned.

"Oh, I suppose you wouldn't know, not coming from California, but they are a small fish that come up to spawn once a year on a full moon. The thing is, they have to come up on the beach and lay their eggs in the sand, and eventually, I guess the tide takes the eggs out to the ocean. So while they are on the sand you can just scoop them up and put them into buckets. They are really little, like sardines, and silver in color, so when they are on the beach, it looks like sparkling silver lights twinkling in the sand."

"That sounds like it would be fun," Lawrence murmured.

"Tons of people come out to catch them. I mean, there are millions of them, and some people camp out on the beach all night to enjoy the adventure. Anyway, my girlfriend had a boyfriend. She was a couple years older than I was, and we all decided to come out and bring another girl, and her boyfriend's best friend, with us. The girl we brought was sort of mentally challenged, if you know what I mean. I think she was about sixteen years old, but she acted more like she was ten years old, so we knew we had to keep a close eye on her."

"Well, that was nice of you to bring her along," Lawrence

commented.

"Really, we brought her with us a lot, because her mother and my girlfriend's boyfriend's mother were friends, so we were always dragging her along, whether we wanted to or not, and this was one night that he didn't want to bring her, because he wanted to be with Jill, my girlfriend, alone on the beach.

"When we got there, we made friends with a group of people that had a bonfire, and we all put our blankets by the fire, but then took off to get the fish, leaving Meg, the tag along, and Rob's friend with her. I went off on my own, because I knew that Jill and Rob wanted to be alone, and I certainly did not want to baby-sit Meg, so I left it up to Rob's friend to watch her.

"To tell you the truth, I was a horrible grunion hunter. I would fill my bucket, and then set it down to get more fish, but then the waves came in and tipped it over, so all my fish would swim away! I was really hopeless," Loraine began to laugh, and Lawrence joined her.

"Finally, after not being able to find more fish to fill my bucket, I headed back to the bonfire, but all the people were gone, except for Rob's friend. I asked him where Meg was, and he just shrugged his shoulders. 'She wandered off with some guy she met,' he told me. 'What?' I screeched. 'You were supposed to be watching her!' He insisted that she wanted to go, and I had to get it into his head that she was like a child, even if she did look like she was sixteen, and no telling what may happen to her! So he and I started looking for her. We ran into Jill and Rob, and by this time, it was about midnight, and we were supposed to be heading home, only we couldn't find Meg. We all walked up and down the beach looking for her, and about two a.m. we all had to call our parents to let them know we would be really late coming home, because we couldn't find Meg.

"Just about the time we were about to call the police, Meg comes wandering up to us, but doesn't say a word about where she had been, or what she had been doing, or even if she was with anyone. She just said she was looking for fish. We didn't get home until about five the next morning, and that is the last time I ever tried to go grunion hunting," Loraine finished.

"Maybe you and I could go grunion hunting sometime," Lawrence suggested. "We could bring your cousin and miss mini skirt," he laughed.

"And then we would be up until five in the morning looking for them," Loraine predicted, as she snuggled a little closer against him.

The feel of her, up against his groin, and her back resting on his chest, filled him with a calm contentment. He was not sexually aroused as much as he was warmly stimulated by the smell of that enticing perfume, and the feel of her body pressing against his. He lifted his hand and slowly pulled the pins from her hair, letting it fall against her shoulders and his chest.

"I love your long hair," he murmured.

"Yes, long hair to men, is like boobs, hips and long legs," she commented. "That is all they see, when looking at a woman."

"Why so cynical? What man treated you wrong?"

Loraine was quiet. No one had treated her wrong, so why did she feel that way about the way a man looked at a woman's body?

When she didn't answer, he just shrugged, and began to absently run his finger against her neck and bare shoulder, as he looked out over the ocean, and nuzzled his cheek against her fragrant hair. He felt her begin to relax, and smiled to himself. It was going to take a lot of melting to get Loraine to let down her barrier, he mused.

He could feel goose bumps forming on her arms, and began to smooth them under his hands to try and warm her. "Are you cold?" he asked her.

"A little, but that is helping," she said, feeling so comfortable that she didn't want to move.

The ocean always had a way of pulling her, calming her, yet making her feel excited and contented at the same time. She drank in its salty smell, and the sound it made as it crashed down on the world. She reached down and removed her sandals, and then pushed her feet down into the still warm sand, at the edge of the blanket, and then snuggled her back a little tighter against Lawrence's hard chest.

The movement she made was causing him to feel aroused, and he tried to ignore the warmth that was spreading through him as he felt himself responding to the closeness of her, and the smell of her, and the feel of her back rubbing against his body the way she was, in order to get comfortable. So he sat as still as he could, while he tried to calm his wild anticipating thoughts. Only his hands still rubbed absently up and down her arms, and he still drank in the sweet smell of her hair, as it fell softly against his cheek. He lowered his head and planted a gentle kiss on the side of her neck, and she gave a little murmur that pushed through him like a fairy's touch. His lips found the edge of her ear, and kissed that as well, and he felt new goose bumps appear on her arms. Lawrence smiled silently and wrapped his arms around her, pulling her even closer against his chest. His arms were resting under her breasts, and he could feel their soft swelling against them. He couldn't resist the urge to kiss her bare shoulder, savoring the salty taste of it. He heard another murmur as his lips pressed against her well-shaped shoulder.

Lawrence was so frightened of scaring her away, that he seemed hesitant to do much more. After all he had promised no more stealing kisses from her, but she had not objected to his touching her with his lips so far. He lowered his knees, and pulled her up onto his lap, to give her more shelter from the wind with his arms, and she pulled her knees up to her chin, as she sat sideways and leaned her head against his shoulder. He continued to stroke the arm that was still exposed to the wind, and as he did so, she reached that arm up around his neck, for better security, as she snuggled into him.

They said nothing, and he just held her against him, savoring the wonderful feeling it was giving him, to have her there, so near to him, without her pulling away, or saying something to distract what he was doing. He stopped for a moment, and removed his jacket, and placed it around her shoulders, pulling her down against him, as he lowered himself on the blanket, with her still nestled against his chest. He now stroked her hair, and back, and he could feel her softly kissing his neck, as she rested her head against his shoulder.

Lawrence closed his eyes like a contented cat, basking in the sun, but the warmth he was soaking in, was just the sunshine of her essence, and the warmth of her body against his. He did not remember when he finally fell asleep, with her snuggled in his arms, breathing softly against his neck.

He was dreaming of being out on a boat in the ocean. He could hear the waves crashing, and he was afraid that it would crash his boat against the shore, but he realized he had a lifejacket on, because it was tied snuggly against him, and it made him feel secure and safe, and then his eyes flew open, and he realized he was laying on the beach, with Loraine in his arms, and the soft dawn starting to seep into the sky above them.

His first impulse was to sit up and wake Loraine up as well, but he restrained himself, as he looked down upon her peacefully sleeping face. He wanted to gaze down on that beautiful face all day, and could not bear to disturb her. He slowly reached his hand over and pushed her hair out of her eyes, and she gave a small whimper, and wrinkled her nose. Her arms clutched him around the neck and pulled his head closer to hers, as she seemed to be trying to get more comfortable. Her nose was touching his cheek, and her lips had pressed against his neck. They moved slightly, and her tongue licked out against her lips, touching his neck as she did so, which shot sparks throughout his body, and he realized how much he wanted her, at that moment.

Lawrence tried to calm himself, and get control of his breathing, which seemed to speed up a little, as he now felt her lips kissing his neck, but her eyes were still closed. Then her face lifted, and he found her lips pressing against his, and he couldn't help himself, as she offered her lips to him, and he pulled them under his own lips as he sucked gently against those pouting lips, and smoothed his tongue against them.

He felt her mouth respond to his, as he pressed his mouth against her lips, and she welcomed the kiss, smoothing her tongue over his lips, causing his loins to go wild. His arms tightened around her, as he hungrily captured her mouth, pulling her body hard against his own throbbing need, and she naturally placed her knee over his leg. He felt her softness through the thin material of her dress, pressing against his own arousal. As they kissed, she moved against him, her body stroking him so tantalizingly that he almost gritted his teeth with the sheer pleasure it gave him.

One hand reached down against her bottom, while the other hand tangled in her hair, pressing her head into his groping kiss. Now both of his hands were holding her firmly against his body, as his head lowered down over the top of her breast. He wanted so much to feel the wonder of her breast against his mouth. The way she was moving against him, encouraged his need, caused him to take a chance and softly kiss against the top of those soft mounds, wanting more of the treasured prize.

Loraine's eyes remained closed, and he was a little astounded that she was willingly allowing him this intimate touch, when she had kept him at such a distance, and had complained about his kisses.

Loraine was dreaming. She was with 'him'. She had crawled out her window and met him on the beach. She loved being with him this way. She loved the way he touched her, and how he made her feel. She wanted him to take her, to touch her, to feel his lips upon her. She would never marry Gaston. Never,

never! He could take her away. They would disappear, and no one would know what became of them. They would spend their lives together, but for now, just the feel of him caused her desire to leap from her body, and she wanted all that he could give her. She could feel his strong chest under her fingers, and his manhood pushing restlessly against her, causing sensations to spiral out of control within her... causing her to want him even more.

Loraine felt his mouth upon her breast, and she wanted him to devour her, to have her in every way he chose. She threw caution to the wind. She turned and offered him her mouth, the very touch of his lips causing her to go wild with desire. She was his! She would always be his! No one could take her from him.

Fate had brought him to her, and now she knew what love was like. How it ached in her body, and pulled at the pit of her stomach, and lifted to her throat, and spread through her heart. And his hands! His beautiful hands were pulling something from her she had never felt before, as they smoothed over her body. His mouth and his hands consumed her, and filled her with need! Her breath caught at what the touch of his hand was doing to her, she wanted even more than just his hand...

She raised her head, she looked down at him as she lifted her mouth from his, his hand was tracing its way up her leg. Suddenly, she gasped, and sprang backwards away from him.

Lawrence was startled as she roughly pulled herself from

him. She had been a wild passionate woman, one moment, and then a startled angry person the next.

"What are you doing?" she almost screamed at him.

"You mean, what were you doing to me? I didn't start this, you know. You started kissing me as though you couldn't get enough of me, and encouraged every touch, every kiss, every…"

She was staring at him in shock, as he spoke, and as her mind cleared, she remembered the dream.

"It…it was not you…it was *him*, I was kissing."

"What are you talking about? It certainly was me you were kissing."

"No…no, I mean I thought…I thought I was her…Loraine of the past, and I was with my lover. I don't know if I had slipped into the past, or if I was dreaming, but I thought I was with him!"

"Lucky fellow!"

He looked at her, not missing the fact that her dress was starting to slip lower, and any farther, her breasts would be exposed completely to his view. When she saw the direction that his eyes took, she looked down and gasped, and then pulled her dress back up, darting daggers with her eyes, back at him.

"I'm sorry. I'm sorry, Loraine. I didn't know you were in some dream of the past. I thought you really wanted me. Sorry I couldn't fill the bill!"

He looked so disappointed, that it touched a soft spot in her heart, and she leaned back against him. "I can't deny that it felt pretty darn good," she smiled.

He pulled her back into his arms. "It felt pretty darn good for me too," he admitted. "You don't think we could pick up where we left off, do you?"

She wanted to, but something held her back. It was that fear again. She wanted him, yet she was afraid to want him. She had some inner awareness that she would discover something horrible if she allowed herself to give in.

"I...I can't. It's that same thing that makes me fear getting close to any man. I almost feel like it has something to do with Loraine of the past. Do you think that maybe I am Loraine from the past, and her memories are what haunt me? Could I have been reincarnated as Loraine of the future, and what happened to her is affecting me in the here and now, as well? Why did she commit suicide? I have to find that out, so I won't be so scared whenever I think about her."

Lawrence tightened his grip. "Don't worry, Loraine. We will get to the bottom of it all, and if you are her reincarnated, then maybe the answers we find will explain to you what is scaring you away from men."

"Well, I don't think it was her lover that made her hate men. It must have been Gaston that frightened her. I know she loved the other man very much. I could feel it so deeply."

"I know." He paused, and took in a heavy breath. "I could see how you felt it, and I can't help but admit that I was feeling it too."

CHAPTER TEN

Loraine picked up the Photo Album that she had set down on the bed when she first found it, and then had placed it on the dresser, when she cleaned the room.

"I have an idea," she said to Lawrence, as she opened the album. "See?" He came over to where she was standing. "It is all her pictures, taken as Loraine grew up, each one dated."

"So? What is that going to do for you? She was even beautiful as a child, you know."

Loraine smiled. "Well, so was I," she laughed, "but what you are missing is her clothes."

"Well, yes, she is wearing clothes." He gave her a steady stare.

"The cloths tell me what she was wearing on that date. If I find the same dresses in her closet, or her trunk, then I can put them on in order according to the album, and if it sends me back in time, maybe it will take me to the date she was wearing the cloths, and I can see what happens as each day advances."

"Yeah, but what if she wears the same thing several times? What if she wore it on a day that she didn't get her pitcher taken, and you go back to that day instead?"

"There is that possibility, but I was also thinking, if I was Loraine back then, I could focus on the picture, when I put on the dress, and make it take me back to the time the picture was taken. Look at this one. It was taken in front of the bank. She is standing between two men. It says 'Me, Father, and Mr. Billings'. We both know who Mr. Billings is. If I can go back to this day, I can find out more about the banker, and what made him try and get her father to force her to marry him, it would unravel a lot of this mystery."

"You may be right."

"I know I am right. Just looking at his picture causes my stomach to churn!"

"Okay, we know how you hate the banker, but we need to make some sort of plan here. You can't just go bouncing in and out of the past and hope everything turns out all hunky dory." Lawrence gave her a frown.

"I was thinking about that as well. And another thing I am worried about. If I leave the house, I may get stuck in time somewhere."

Lawrence nodded. "That could be a problem, but as long as you keep your clothes on, you will probably remain in that time, but you know you will always come back home to go to bed, so then when you remove your clothes, you should end up here in this room again."

"What if I have to go to visit someone and have to stay the night? If I take my clothes off, I will turn up in some strange house, if it still exists in this day, and maybe in bed with some stranger!"

Lawrence gave a small laugh. "Yes, I know how you would hate that to happen!"

"I am being serious, here." Loraine wrinkled her nose and glared at him.

"Just don't take your clothes off except when you are in this room. Then you will know that you can get back right here safe and sound."

"I don't even know if it will still work. It might have just been a fluke, because it was her wedding dress, and she had such strong emotions about not marrying Gaston that I was swept back in time to protest against it."

"The only way to find out is to try it," Lawrence encouraged.

"I am almost afraid, having to relive something that Loraine of the past hated."

"But she is not reliving it. It only happened once to her. It is you who is just visiting it. I bet if you put that wedding dress on again, you would go back to that same day, and do the exact same thing she did the first time you went back."

"Ok then, let's try it." She went to the wardrobe and took

the wedding dress out. "Close your eyes, so I can change into it."

"I thought the whole point of me coming with you is to see what happens when you put the dress on. If I can't watch you put the dress on, how am I going to know what happens? Besides, I am sure you will keep your underwear on, so what are you afraid of me looking at?"

Loraine turned pink and turned her back to him, and he grinned broadly at her embarrassment. She gave a little growl in her throat and started taking her jeans off, and then her shirt, with her back still turned to him.

"Very nice looking ass you have there," he teased.

"If you are going to watch, keep your thoughts to yourself!" she hissed.

"Yes, my lady," he responded in a proper tone of voice that let her know how unrealistic she was being.

However, his thoughts did go a little crazy as he took in her slim bare waist, and her lace panties, and when she bent over to pull her jeans down, he almost lost his own composure, and thought of reaching out and touching that lovely bottom, that was making his heart speed. Loraine pulled the dress over her head, and nothing much happened. She was fumbling with the buttons, and Lawrence automatically stepped forward and started buttoning them up for her. He hoped it didn't change how things worked taking her back to the past, if he did that, but she didn't stop him.

Once she had the dress on, and it was all buttoned, Loraine suddenly collapsed onto the floor. Shocked, Lawrence went to her, and grabbed her hand. If felt cold, but she had a strong pulse. She was mumbling something, and he put his ear near her mouth to listen.

"I won't be long mother," she was saying.

Lawrence suddenly realized, that when Loraine went back in time, it was not her body that left, but some essence of her, reliving that past life, and the dress was what triggered the memory and caused her to pass into another dimension of time, he figured. She was so cold, that he pulled back the spread on the bed, lifted her up and laid her in it, then covered her up.

No sooner had he laid her on the bed, when she sat up and jumped out of the bed, and walked over to the wardrobe, and pulled out the yellow dress, laying it on the bed. Then she started removing the wedding dress, but her eyes were just staring blankly while she was doing it, like a sleep walker. When the dress fell to the floor, Loraine blinked, and then saw Lawrence standing there, staring at her.

"You were right," she breathed, "I did go back to the same time, and everything that happened then, happened again in the same way. So I must just be reliving experiences, triggered by the clothes she wore at the time."

"Not only that, but you didn't go anywhere. Your body

remained here, but you just collapsed like you had fallen asleep, only I could hear you talking. It must be like having a dream, or a recall of memory of that time, and you see everything in your mind while it is happening, but the Loraine of today, remains here, while Loraine of the past sees herself doing other things. This means that you won't get stuck in some house, if you take your clothes off other than in this room. You will just come back to your body here and wake up in this room."

"That's a relief, but it all seemed so real, and how did the dress get on the bed?"

"You got up and put it there, sort of like sleep walking. I had placed you on the bed because you were so cold, but no sooner did I do that, when you jumped up and went over to the closet and took out the dress, laid it on the bed, and started taking the wedding dress off."

"So what would happen if I decide to go sleepwalking through the house for some reason while I am in the past in my head, but my body wants to do something? Like climbing out the window to go find my lover."

"That would create a problem. So I think it would be safer if I stayed here with you, every time you go back to the past. And we will keep the door locked. And I won't let you climb out the window. If you try to go out the door, or try to unlock it, I will stop you from doing that too."

"I guess that should work."

Loraine realized as she was talking to Lawrence that she was still standing there in her panties and bra, and she hadn't even thought about it. She had actually felt comfortable just standing there like that talking to him.

Lawrence, however, was at his wits end, trying to distract himself from the way she looked with her hair hanging over her shoulders down to her waist, and the fact that her lace bra and lace panties were practically see through, and he could feel himself starting to remember how nice she felt in his arms, when they had been at the beach.

For a moment, they just stared at each other. She was looking at him strangely, as though she was trying to see something. It was almost as if she were looking right through him. Without saying anything, she walked up to him, and placed her hand on his cheek, but kept staring into his eyes. He noticed her chest rising and falling, as her breath started to speed up, and she had a questioning look in her eyes.

Lawrence was afraid to move, in case he broke the spell, so he just stood there to see what she did next. What she did next, was exactly what she had done at the beach. She stood up on her toes, and placed a kiss on his mouth... a very gentle kiss. He decided not to respond, just to see what she was going to do next. As she kissed him, her arms came up around his neck, and her soft lace clad body pressed up against him, causing his senses to go stark raving mad. He was afraid to put his arms around her waist, the way he wanted to, and wondered how long it would take her to come out of the daze? Apparently she was back in time, and she hadn't even put on any of Loraine's old clothes. What was triggering this, he wondered?

"You shouldn't be in my room," she breathed against his neck, and then kissed the place where her lips were pressed.

He didn't know whether he should answer her or not. Was whoever she thought she was with, talking to her as well, he wondered? He decided not to say anything, unless she pressed the point. So he stood there, trying to keep his hands off of her, but she was pressing so hard against his body, it was causing havoc throughout his senses.

"We should lock the door, in case anyone should discover you here. It's late, but still someone may be up." The key was still in the door, and she walked over and tried to turn it, even though they had locked the door when they first entered the room. "Oh, I see you have already locked it," she smiled, and then returned to him, placing her arms around his neck again, and lifting her head to him, as if expecting him to kiss her, so he did. The moment his lips touched hers, he felt his own arms reach around her waist, pulling her against his body, once again, and she did not resist. God, what was going to happen when she woke out of this dream?

Would she hate him? Should he wake her up? Yes, that is what he should do, is wake her up. He put his hands on her shoulder and gave her a shake. She stiffened.

"Why are you shaking me? Are you angry with me, for some reason? What did I do?"

"Wake up, Loraine," he said urgently.

"I am not asleep. I know it is late, but I couldn't sleep, and then you came in. You must have known I was thinking of you."

He kissed her hard on the mouth, hoping that the roughness of the kiss would break her out of her dream, but instead, she merely responded to his kiss, pushing her body even closer against his.

Damn! He couldn't be alone with this girl without her thinking he was her lost lover from the past, and if she woke up in his arms, she would blame him! He could walk out, but that would be cruel, and then there was the possibility that she would try to follow him, dressed only in her panties and bra. Loraine must have really loved that guy, and in some mysterious way, he had taken the place of that lost lover in her fogged memory of the past.

He pulled his mouth away and stood staring down at her. "God, you're beautiful," he groaned.

"You're beautiful too," she breathed, and he realized that her fingers were unbuttoning his shirt, and then her hands smoothed over his hard chest, and her mouth was kissing his chest, licking against his skin, and he gave a little gasp, as a flame shot straight to his neither regions.

"Loraine...uh...I don't think you should be doing this," he breathed, as his heart started to race.

"Father and Mother are gone. No one will catch us. I don't know why you are so worried. It's not like you have never touched me before."

Apparently this was not the first time she had been with him. "When did I touch you before?" he asked in a husky voice, hoping to learn something about her lover.

"Don't you remember? On the beach, how could you forget?"

"I didn't forget, I just wanted to make sure you had not forgotten how wonderful it was," and he thought to himself that was the truth. It had been wonderful while it lasted. He wondered how long this would last, and that is what frightened him.

She was removing his shirt, and he didn't know whether to embrace the situation, and her, or resist it. Apparently he was not going to wake her up, or she would have woken up by now. She was actually carrying on a conversation with him, so nothing he said would make a difference to her, he figured. And he certainly did not want to hurt the Loraine of the past, and that woman of the past wanted a piece of him.

"Touch me," she whispered, as she looked up into his eyes.

"Touch me the way you did on the beach. It felt so good!"

"Yes it did," he murmured, wishing he really had been able to touch her more than what he had done on the beach, but hesitated, and she took his hand and placed it on her breast.

"You can have me," she told him boldly. "I want you. It's not like we haven't been in each other's arms before. Why are you being so hesitant?"

Lawrence's breath came out in a rush, as his heart pounded against his ribs, begging him to comply with her wishes. "I want you too," he whispered, as he took her mouth against his again, hoping to distract her from this seduction by just participating in kissing her. He deepened his kiss in hopes that she would be satisfied with the sensations it gave her, and hopefully wake up soon. But she took his other hand and placed it on her stomach.

"Touch me the way you did on the beach. Touch all of me," she begged.

He stood there, one hand on her breast, and one on her stomach, and she was practically raping him with her mouth, as she kissed him with a passion he had never experienced before with any other woman, which had been few, he had to admit. Yet, this woman in his arms... This wonderful woman in his arms, who wasn't of this world, he realized, was doing something to him that could wear down a stronger man than himself. Amelia had some mother, he exclaimed to himself.

He moved his hand down slowly, timidly under the lace at his fingertips, feeling the soft curls clustered there, and he herd her sigh. Oh how he wanted to just push his hand farther, find the softness of her, and explore to his heart's content, but he restrained himself still. He felt like he would be violating her, since she really wasn't aware of what she was doing. And if she was, it was in some other time and place. If he could just content her with…with…kisses were not doing the trick, he admitted, because she kept demanding more.

He lowered her to the bed. He would just hold her, kiss her, and hope she fell asleep for real in that past life. She willingly came into his arms, as he lie with her on the bed, stroking her hair, and kissing those soft pliable lips.

"Please," she pouted. "I want more than just kisses from you. You wanted me on the beach, and you came to my room, so why are you holding back?"

"I don't want to hurt you, Loraine," he told her.

"It didn't hurt before. Why should it hurt now?"

He knew the Loraine of the past must have been a virgin back then, and had her lover had sex with her, there would have been some pain involved. Apparently they had not had actual intercourse, and he wasn't going to do that now, either. For all he knew, because of Loraine's strange fear of men, she was probably still a virgin, and he was not about to discover it one way or the other, while she seemed to be trying to seduce him in her sleep.

But Loraine had placed his hand against her again, offering herself to him. Practically demanding he take her, and he certainly wanted to touch her, to make her soar with pleasure, even if that was the only thing he did, and he found his hand complying with her wishes. He couldn't stop his mouth from searching for the softness of her breasts, his free hand pulling the strap of her bra over her shoulder to expose one to him. And then the other strap, and the hooks in back were undone, and the pretty lace thing fell away, allowing him to drink her in with his eyes, and then drink her in with his mouth, as his fingers pushed that other lacy thing over her long luscious legs. And there she lay on the bed, fully exposed to his searching eyes, and his wanting mouth, and his eager hands, yet he was still afraid she would wake up and then never talk to him again.

She gave a little mew, and stretched enticingly before him, and he gave in. His mouth hesitantly explored her inviting skin, finding every inch of her, tasting the flavor of her, causing his will to weaken even more. He wanted all of her... wanted to touch all of her, not leaving a part to his imagination. But his better judgment was starting to get a hold of his wayward actions.

Instead, he restrained himself, and pulled her softly into his arms, as he marveled at her brazen actions, and still she had not woken up from her extraordinary sleep. Feeling self-conscience, he gently put her lacy things back on her, and covered her with the spread, and lay beside her, waiting for her to come out of her daze, while he stroked her hair, and hoped she would not remember anything beyond removing her dress.

After about a half hour, when he was almost dozing, she moved, and lifted her head, looking into his face. "What happened? Did I fall asleep?"

"Yeah, sort of, you might say that."

"I was having a wonderful dream."

"Really?"

"Why didn't you wake me up?"

"I tried to. Believe me, I tried too."

"The dream was too good to be awoken from."

"So what did you dream?" he asked with a sly smile.

"Oh, it was heavenly…and…" She blinked.

"I hope it was," he said, "I finally gave in and lay down with you."

"I can see that."

Then she surprised him and turned and kissed him. "Thank you for not waking me up."

He looked at her puzzled. "Do you remember what you were dreaming?"

"Yes. I was in his arms again. He was making me feel so good. Only it didn't feel like a dream. He seemed so real to me."

"Well, I'm right here, and I'm real," he suggested hopefully.

"We are forgetting what we came here for," she reminded.

"No, *you* forgot what we came her for, and started having a heavenly dream."

"Yeah, it was kind of funny. One moment I was talking to you, and the next thing I knew, I was having the dream that he came into my room and... Well I won't go into it, but he had magical hands and his mouth, I definitely loved his mouth."

"Really, and you can't enlighten me?"

"I would be too embarrassed to," she told him truthfully.

"After all we have been through together?"

She just looked at him, grabbed her shirt off of the bed, and pulled it over her head, then wriggled into her jeans.

"Why are you putting your clothes on? I thought you were going to try another one of Loraine's dresses?"

"Yes, yes, I was. I wanted to put on the dress that she was wearing in that picture in front of the bank, and see what I learned."

"Sounds like a good place to start," he agreed, "now that you have had your beauty sleep."

Loraine peered at the dress in the photograph of Loraine in front of the bank, and then rummaged through the closet, but could not find the dress. She turned to the trunk at the end of the bed, and started pulling clothes out of it.

"I think this is the one. What do you think?" She held it up to herself.

"Looks like the right dress, but do me a favor. Sit on the bed once you put it on, and don't stand up. If you go back to the past, you can just lie down, and I won't have to worry about you falling down and hitting your head or something."

"Good idea," she mumbled. She pulled off her jeans, as she sat on the edge of the bed.

"Need any help?" he asked with a broad grin, bringing the dimple out from hiding.

She just glared at him, and then pulled her shirt off, as he watched on. She didn't even try to hide herself from him. Apparently she had gotten beyond her shyness of him looking at her lovely body, barely clad, and she just reached for the dress, and pulled it over her head. Lawrence helped her, without asking, seeing as how it had a bunch of buttons at the back as well, and he was sure she would never be able to reach them all. The dress was a little tattered. The lace at the front bodice had been ripped, and also the lace at one of the sleeves, but it looked very stunning on her, with its green stripes, and its ruffled collar, and puffed sleeves.

As soon as the dress was buttoned, Lawrence pushed her back onto the bed, and made her sit down, just as she got a dazed look on her face, and then closed her eyes. He helped her lay back against the pillow, and watched anxiously.

"Hello, father," he heard her say so softly he could barely hear her. He pulled a chair up to the bed and sat, gazing at her, and trying to pick up on her conversation.

"There you are, sweetheart. Are you ready to go?"

Loraine looked at this man, who was very good looking for his age, with graying hair at his temples, but still in good shape otherwise, and realized it was her father, or the father of her 'other self'. It had worked. The dress had taken her back in time, and she realized that her father was wearing the same clothes she had seen him wearing in the photograph in Loraine's album. She knew she was about to meet the banker.

"Someday you and your future husband will be taking over the business, so it is about time you learn about the finances. I am going to make a deposit at the bank, and I want you to meet Mr. Billings, who is president of the bank. Things are going pretty well for us, and when I am gone, you and your family will be very well off, if you keep things running smoothly."

"I know nothing about business matters, father. What good is all this going to do?"

"Your future husband will have to learn the business, but until you marry, you have to have a little knowledge of what is done. I know you know everything about making shoes, since you practically lived at the factory when you were little, but that is not the only thing there is to learn. The shoes have to be sold once they are made, and the money has to be managed efficiently to keep the business remaining a lucrative concern."

Loraine was nervous, as her father steered her to the front door. She wasn't sure she wanted to step out of the house, and hesitated at the front door, as her father held it open for her.

"What are you waiting for? The carriage is waiting, and I don't have all day."

Loraine looked out over the front porch, down the stairs to the street below and saw a horse and carriage standing there, waiting for them. This seemed to excite her, since she had never ridden in a carriage before. It was all it took to get her to step over the threshold and follow her father down the steps. The dress she had put on was now new, the torn lace a thing of the past, or the future, she thought. There were petticoats beneath it, pushing out the skirt, and she liked the feel of the satin and lace against her legs. She realized she was wearing pantalets, and sheer white stockings, held up with a garter. It made Loraine feel kind of sad that they no longer dressed this way, and she started to enjoy her laps back into the past.

Loraine's father helped her up into the carriage, and then sat beside her, signaling the driver to proceed, and the horses turned their beautiful sleek heads, and the carriage followed, and headed down the road in the direction of the bank, Loraine assumed.

She recognized the bank from the picture in the album, and a man at the door held it open for them. Imagine having a door man at a bank, or maybe he was a security guard in disguise. She smiled at him, as she held her father's elbow and passed into the bank. When the clerk saw them enter, he seemed excited.

"Right this way," he instructed, as he opened another door, and they were now standing inside of a large office-looking room.

The man behind the desk, lifted his head, and as soon as he did, Loraine took an involuntary step backwards. He looked her up and down, as though he was taking her clothes off with his eyes, then rose and walked around the desk, with his hand extended to her father.

"So nice to see you, Mr. Landon!" he said shaking hands with her father, "and this must be your lovely daughter, you have been telling me about. Getting ready to learn about business expenses and how to do the deposits, are you?" he asked turning towards Loraine, and giving a half bow.

She just nodded, hating the sight of the man, but knowing she must be polite. If it had of been in her own time, she probably would have turned, and told her father she would wait for him outside. But instinctively she knew that would be rude in this other time frame, so she stood her ground.

"Sit down, sit down," The banker pulled up another chair to

his desk, and helped Loraine seat herself, and her father sat in a chair that was already before the desk. Then, Mr. Billings returned to the other side of the desk.

"I have been going over your files, Mr. Landon, and I am pleased to see everything in the black, and that your company is making a very large profit. I hope your family's New York store is doing as well as yours, here in San Diego."

"I don't keep track of their business, though at the end of the year, we do have to reveal our books to each other. I let my manager take care of all that."

"As it should be, as it should be." He nodded to Loraine. "I must say you have a most beautiful daughter. I am surprised she has not been spoken for by now."

"She is very particular about who she allows to call on her," he glanced towards his daughter. Loraine could tell by the look in his eye that it seemed to irk him that she was still single. She realized that in that day and age, she was beyond marriageable age, and her father had spoken of a future husband helping her take over the business. Since he did not have a son, it must have been very important to him, for her to get married, and apparently, she had been putting it off.

"My dear wife died several years ago," Mr. Billings informed them. "It is lonely without a woman around the house. Any man would be proud to call Miss Landon his wife, I am sure."

"Well, apparently she is not proud to call any man her husband," Mr. Landon said with a nervous chuckle, "but hopefully, she will find a suitable mate, in the near future."

"Father, I thought you brought me here to show me the financial end of the business. Not talk about my single condition, and my impending husband, in some far distant future," she rebuffed.

"So I did. So I did. Sorry, Loraine, I got distracted." Loraine felt he knew it had been rude of him to speak of her like that in front of Mr. Billings, but she believed he did it on purpose to make her pointedly aware of his impatience for her to choose a husband.

Mr. Landon proceeded with his business, but the whole time, Loraine realized that the banker could not keep his eyes off of her, and it made her very nervous. When the dealings were over with, Loraine let out a breath of relief, but was brought up short when Mr. Billings rose and put his hand on her waist, after pulling back her chair.

"My photographer happens to be in today and I would like him to take a photograph of us in front of the bank to use for public relations, you understand. A photo of me with my satisfied customers would be good advertisement, if you have no objections. I will give you a copy when it is developed."

"I have no objections," Loraine's father said, glancing at

her. She did not look happy, but business was business, and he ignored it.

Mr. Billings positioned her between the two of them and made a point of placing his hand on her back as the photographer snapped the pitcher. Loraine could not force herself to smile, even though she was encouraged to do so. As they started to turn away, Mr. Billings called to her father.

"May I speak with you a moment?" He pulled Mr. Landon aside and Loraine busied herself by walking to the shop next to the bank, and gazing into the window at the merchandise.

Shortly, her father joined her and they got into the carriage. "Mr. Billings seemed rather enamored by you," he said, and she frowned.

"I could care little what Mr. Billings thought about me," she responded, thinking the very name made her feel faint.

"He asked me if he could come calling on you," her father continued.

She turned her head sharply and stared at him. "Certainly not!" she spat the words without even thinking.

"He is very well-to-do. Has plenty of money, and would be an asset to the business. He would make a fine son-in-law."

"He would make a terrible husband! I have no attraction to him whatsoever. He makes my stomach crawl!" Loraine almost bellowed.

"I am sorry you feel that way," her father frowned.

"Please tell Mr. Billings, the next time you see him, that I have no interest in allowing him to call on me, ever! Thank him kindly for the offer though," she smiled sweetly.

"I hope you know what you are doing. Mr. Billings does not seem like the sort that would take no for an answer."

"Mr. Billings is probably twice my age. He must have a very huge ego to believe I would simper at his offer to call on me. Besides he is ugly!"

"That is quite rude. He has very good features."

"His soul is ugly. I could feel it crawling all over me every time his eyes looked at me." Loraine gave a shudder.

"You are imagining things," her father brushed it aside.

"Nevertheless, I shall have none of Mr. Billings, and you can tell him that for me, father," Loraine insisted.

The carriage arrived at the house, and Loraine jumped down without waiting for her father to help her, and ran up the steps of the house, and straight to her room. She started pulling the dress off, as soon as she closed the door. She tore at the lace and heard it rip. She hated that dress. She would never wear it again, she told herself, because it would remind her of the way Mr. Billings had looked at her.

Lawrence watched Loraine tearing at her clothes, and he started undoing the buttons to help her. She seemed agitated, as though she could not wait to have the dress off of her. As soon as he helped her pull it over her head, she threw it to the floor, and started breathing heavily, as she seethed in the anger, she was still feeling.

"Calm down! It was only in the past. What happened? I only heard small parts of your conversation, as you mumbled in your sleep," Lawrence encouraged, as he tried to calm her down.

"I hate him. I *hate* him! He was drooling over me! It was insulting!" She turned and looked at Lawrence, as her eyes brimmed with tears.

He naturally reached out and pulled her against him, holding her tight. "It was not *you* he was drooling over, Loraine. You have to learn to separate yourself from the Loraine of the past. If this is going to upset you so much, maybe you shouldn't do it anymore," he suggested.

"I have to do it. I have to. I can't give up just because I don't like what is happening. She was me, Lawrence. Don't you understand that? I have to know what happened to me back then that ruined my life!"

"But that was in the past, Loraine. How can it have so much effect on you now? I know how important all of this is for you, in order to help Amelia, but you need to stop taking it all so seriously," he comforted, as he pat her back, and held her against his shoulder, while she shook in his arms.

For such a sassy girl, she had her vulnerable moments, he thought, and wished she trusted him more. Loraine suddenly pulled away.

"But don't you understand, Lawrence? If I am that Loraine of the past, that means I am Amelia's mother! That's why I have to do this. I must have come here for a reason, and that is why I was always drawn to the house. I left my daughter in the past to a father who had done something to me, that caused me to take my life. I owe it to Amelia to discover why that Loraine, of the past, would rather end her life, than remain here and raise her daughter.

"I hadn't thought of that," Lawrence breathed. "Wow, this is hard to grasp. I am Amelia's distant cousin, but you may be her distant mother."

"Well, we won't break it to her until this mystery is solved. She may not even believe in reincarnation. I don't even know if I do. But all of this seems so real, it must have happened the way I am discovering, every time I put on one of Loraine's dresses.

"Just don't let it get to you so much," Lawrence advised. But he knew she probably wouldn't listen to him.

CHAPTER ELEVEN

Amelia smiled at the two across from her at the dinner table. "You two are so busy nowadays, I hardly see you anymore," she said, a little sadly.

"The garden is a lot of work," Lawrence told her, which was true, but a lot of his time was spent with Loraine, trying to discover things from the past.

"But we did manage to find out some things about why the business was going under after the fire." Loraine plowed into the story about what happened after the fire, and how the orders kept getting lost. "And that banker has something to do with it, I am sure, since your grandfather kept taking out loans with him in order to get things back to normal again. And Mr. Billings wanted to call on Loraine, but she would have none of him."

"How do you know she would have none of him?" Amelia asked. "Did you find her diary?"

Loraine looked at Lawrence, and then back at Amelia. "No, I didn't find her diary, but if I do, you will be the first to find out about it."

"But if you haven't gotten into the room, how can you find her diary?" Amelia wanted to know.

"I mean when I get into the room and find her diary."

"So how do you know she wouldn't let the banker call on her?"

"She disappeared on her wedding day, and when they found her, the wedding was called off." Loraine tried to explain.

"That doesn't mean anything. The Banker could have called off the wedding for some reason himself."

"I just have this feeling. The banker was so much older than she was. She would never want to marry him."

"How do you know the banker was older than her," Amelia asked. "Is there something you are not telling me?"

"Yes." Loraine said at last. "I am psychic. I keep having flashbacks about your mother. You know like a psychic does when trying to solve a murder. I seem to know things about her, and I know she hated that banker."

"You are really psychic?" Amelia raised her eyebrows and stared at Loraine. "I hope what you are feeling is the truth though. How can you tell?"

"When we find her diary, we will find out, won't we?"

"I suppose so. I'm glad I hired you. Imagine being psychic. That makes you just the person to help me learn more about my mother."

"Yes," Loraine said under her breath. "Just the person to help you learn more about your mother," and she sat stock still as she thought about the fact that if she truly *was* Loraine of the past, then this woman sitting before her was her daughter of the past. The daughter she never got the chance to raise. She had killed herself rather than tell her daughter the truth about herself, whatever that was. And now she was here in her daughter's house, a house she used to live in herself, trying to help her unravel the mystery. Perhaps Loraine of the past repented of not staying and raising her daughter, after she killed herself, and had come back to make it up to her. It seemed to be the only answer. Now she had to discover the truth, even if the truth turned out to be something very painful. She only hoped Amelia would be strong enough to accept it, if that was the case.

"Well, I guess you flubbed that up," Lawrence said to her as they left the dining room together.

"I had to tell her something. I feel bad that I can't be honest with her, but until I find out the truth, I don't want her getting too excited about everything. I don't know how long we are going to hold her off, and not tell her we got into the room," Loraine grumbled. "I feel terrible, but I don't want to tell her anything until the whole story comes to light."

"Yeah, we don't want her having a heart attack over anything, do we?" Lawrence gave her a serious look.

"Her mother committing suicide is not just anything!" Loraine pointed out.

"Perhaps you have bitten off more than you can chew." He scrutinized her.

Loraine ignored his statement. "I was thinking, when I was talking to her, that if I am her mother from the past, it may be hard to explain it to her. But like I told you, I must have needed to come back here because I must have regretted killing myself, and wanted to make it up to her somehow. Why else would I be drawn to this house all my life, and end up coming here, and her hiring me because I had the same name as her mother? I left her with my horrible father, who never mentioned my name again, or let her know anything about me. Only, apparently, he never told her the truth about herself either. That is the worse. I left it up to him to tell her, and he never did. It was his fault she ended up in that wheelchair, and could never have a normal life."

"Don't you think you are taking this all too seriously?" Lawrence mumbled.

He wasn't sure she was Loraine of the past. Maybe she was having these strange insights for some reason, but it could be because she was so obsessed with the story, her name was Loraine, just like Amelia's mother, and she wanted to help the old woman discover something about her mother.

"I can't help it. When I go back in time, I know it is me remembering those things. I don't think I am going back in time at all. I think I am just having memories of my past, but they are so buried that I have to make them come back to me, by putting on her clothes. I am sure the vibrations of her remain on those clothes, and they seep into me, when I put them on, and make me remember."

"Then how do you account for you mistaking me for your lover, when you were not wearing her clothes?"

"That was just a dream, Lawrence. People remember their past in their dreams too, I am told. I have been reading up on reincarnation at the library, and there are lots of ways that people start to remember past lives."

"Okay, I believe that perhaps Loraine of the past could be you, considering you are the spitting image of her, but your memory is being triggered by other things besides her clothes," he informed her. He decided he needed to get it off his chest in case it happened again.

"What things? I told you all the things I remember from that life so far."

"But I have not told you other things you remember, when we are alone together."

She gave him a puzzled look. "The only time we were alone together was at the beach, and that was a dream. A dream that was a little too real for my comfort."

"That isn't the only time you have dreamed, Loraine. When we were in the locked room, you started dreaming without lying down and going to sleep. In fact, you practically jumped my bones in that room. Actually, you *did* jump my bones in that room and you kept begging me to make love to you. You even said we had done it at the beach, and asked me why I was holding you off?"

"What?"

Think hard, Loraine. What was the dream you were having when you woke up in my arms that day?"

"Oh…oh…YOU!... It was *you*?"

"No, it was your lover of the past, which you made me into! I tried to wake you up, and you would not stop throwing yourself at me. I would have left, but you were half dressed, and I was afraid you would leave the room like that in your sleepwalking state, so I stayed there. You begged me to take you! You really know how to turn a guy on, Loraine, and I was irrevocably turned on. I can't deny it. I was afraid you would wake up at any minute and slap me in the face!"

"Oh, you can't tell me that I forced you!" she fumed.

"Shh! Let's go back up there and we'll talk about it. It's the only place we won't be disturbed."

She followed him up the stairs, and handed him the key, which she kept on her person at all times. She walked in and flounced down on the bed, staring at him with angry eyes.

"Now tell me how I practically raped you," she insisted,

folding her arms across her chest.

"Stand up." he said.

"Why?"

"Just do what I tell you. You won't believe me, so I am going to show you."

"What? You are using this as an excuse to..."

"Like heck I am! I don't want you accusing me of taking advantage of you. If I show you, you will remember the dream, and know you encouraged me, you begged me, you practically forced me!"

She pushed out her lower lip and stood up. "Okay, I am standing."

"Then walk over here, real slow." She obeyed. "Ok, now look into my eyes. Look deeply into my eyes."

She lifted her eyes and looked at him. Her eyes were wide, and she stared at him, before he said anything more, she reached her arms up around his neck. He grabbed them and threw them down.

"Don't you start it again, Loraine, try to keep hold of your senses."

She blinked up at him. "I...I was doing it again?"

"Not quite, but you were about to. Do you see how quickly it comes on? There is something that is triggering this in you. Either you are starved for a man's touch, or you flip out every time you look into my eyes, and think I am your long lost lover."

"Why would I think that?"

"Beats me, but you do. You said I had come into your room. Your parents were out, and you wanted me to touch you the way I did on the beach."

"I never said that!" Her eyes narrowed, thinking he was just trying to get beyond her resisting him, all the time.

"You certainly did," Lawrence insisted. "Try to remember the dream, Loraine."

She closed her eyes. Misty thoughts seemed to clutter them... misty thoughts of him touching her, kissing her, but it wasn't Lawrence, it was him...him of the past, and she didn't know what his name was. Yet, certainly she had not forced him to do anything to her.

Loraine opened her eyes. "You can't make a man make love to you, even though a man can force himself on a woman," she said stubbornly.

"No, you can't make him, but you can sure encourage him! You took my hand, don't you remember?" He placed her hand on his wrist, and then brought it to her breast. "You took it and placed in right here, only then you just had that skimpy little thing you call a bra on, so sheer, so soft, so revealing..."

She jerked his hand away. "I did not!"

"You certainly did! And then if that was not enough," he

took her other hand and placed it on his other wrist, placing his hand back on her breast, and then placing the other on her stomach. "You took the other hand and placed it right here, while my first hand was resting so sweetly there..."

"I would never do that," she whispered with a strained voice.

"But Loraine of the past definitely did! And you had on those lacy little panties, and begged me to touch you the way whoever you thought it was, had done on the beach."

She had not removed his hands as she had before and he stood before her with one hand on her breast and the other on her stomach.

"Those hands, those beautiful hands! I remember thinking...those...Oh!" She suddenly pulled away from him.

"Oh, yes, it *was* sweet. Wonderfully sweet, while I worried the whole time you would wake up and go berserk all over me! But man, you smelled so good, and you felt so good, and you kept telling me to touch you, and that you wanted me. And by gum, I wanted you too. Only, I swear, Loraine, I didn't do any more than touch you. But it was mighty hard not to give in to more than just touching you, the way you kept begging me for more!"

Loraine turned from him, and put her hands over her eyes. "Oh, oh, oh. This is terrible. You were supposed to be here to keep me from doing anything stupid! And you...you..."

"I tried to wake you up. I shook you. I told you we shouldn't be doing anything, but Loraine of the past was mad about me. She loved me, she wanted me. She did everything but …" He walked to her and put his arms around her. "Don't take it like that. What we shared was beautiful, even if you thought I was someone else. You were still Loraine of today, to me, and I wanted to make you feel pleasure from my touch. I wanted you to be happy I touched you that way. I loved the way you were touching me back…no I did not take my clothes off…" he added as he felt her stiffen, "but I would never change that moment. I couldn't stand hiding it from you, so that is why I've told you, in case it ever happens again, you will be forewarned."

"I feel so stupid!" Loraine shuddered.

He turned her in his arms, and pulled her hands away from her face. "You are not stupid. You are beautiful. You have nothing to be ashamed of. I wanted you, I still want you, but I would never do anything like that without you willingly wanting me to do it, and in your frame of mind at the time, you wanted *him* to do it, so I became *him* for you."

She was very still as she stood there, with his hands on her shoulders, looking down into her troubled face.

"Give it up, Loraine, and accept it. You liked it, I liked it. You said it was a heavenly dream. I am glad you thought it was heavenly. I thought it was heavenly, and I would do it again,

Loraine. By God, I would do it all again."

"Why do you trigger that in me?" She stopped and gasped. "Maybe you are not the only one that triggers it in me. I have had this terrible crush on Randy! Did I think he was my lost love as well? My own cousin?"

"Did you force your affections on him?"

"We kissed once, but then realized it was all wrong, but it didn't change my strong attraction towards him."

"And yet all other men seem to turn you off."

"That's right."

"Well, I, for one, am glad I do not turn you off," he whispered, and lowered his lips to hers.

Loraine kissed him absently, as she tried to let what he had told her sink in. He kissed her eagerly, since she did not resist.

"You said, when you woke up, that you wished it had not been a dream. I would like to experience that all again, with you in the here and now, and see if you respond in the same way, as the Loraine of the past did."

She didn't say anything, and he took a chance, and lifted the edge of her shirt, and slowly began to pull it over her head. At first she stood firm, but then she found herself lifting her arms, allowing him to remove the shirt.

Lawrence looked down at the skimpy little bra, and smiled. He reached his fingers to her jeans, and undid the button, and then pulled on the zipper, pushing them down over her hips wondering if maybe he was expecting more than she was willing to give? Only she was not resisting, as they fell in a heap on the floor, and she stepped out of them.

"Yes, just your skimpy little bra, and your pretty lace panties," he breathed, but he didn't move for a very long time.

Then timidly Loraine reached her hand up, and took his hand and placed it on her breast, and then the other, she placed on her stomach, and he smiled, allowing the dimple to wink from his cheek, in his pleasure. He picked her up, and placed her on the bed, removing one strap to her bra, and then the other, just as he had done before. Pulling it slowly away, to once again view her breasts, but this time she did not think he was 'him'. She knew who he was, he hoped. The panties came next, and he pulled them slowly over her legs, taking his time as he took in the beauty of her body.

"But your shirt was off," she said softly. "I remember your shirt was off."

"So it was, but you took it off of me," he reminded her.

Loraine sat up, and as she undid the buttons, he released the hooks on her bra. And they sat and looked at each other, not speaking, merely letting their eyes take the other in. Lawrence watched Loraine's hand creep out, and timidly rest on the waist band of his jeans, then in one simple move flipping the button free.

"I don't think that was part of the dream," he breathed, as his heart raced uncontrollably.

"This isn't the dream," she said, as she lowered the zipper.

"You sure you want to do this? I know you're a virgin, Lorain, I wouldn't want to..."

"Just touching, Lawrence. I'm sort of new to this, since you are the only one..." She took in her breath. "Just touching," she repeated, "so I can get used to this."

He understood, and he wanted her touch, as much as he wanted to touch her. The jeans escaped his body, and he lowered himself beside her as the touching began.

Loraine had never allowed any man to touch her as intimately as she was allowing Lawrence to do, and she had never touched a man the way she was touching him. She had been frightened at first, waiting for that panicky feeling to flood through her, but it did not come, and then she forgot all about it, when the things he was doing to her, caused her to gasp and revel in the moment of sheer excitement. She wasn't thinking of 'him' that man of her past that she couldn't remember the name of. She was caught up with Lawrence, the man in her here and now who was being so tender, and considerate, in the way he used his hands and mouth on her body.

His touches, inspired her own desire to touch him as well, and she wanted him to experience that same earth shattering wonder, that was pouring through her, created by the mere touch of his hand, or the soft kissing of his lips, and subtle tasting with his tongue. She matched his every action, as he introduced her body to what pleasures a man's touch could give to her. Her breath caught, and his breath caught only moments after. She moaned in pleasure, and he was soon moaning in the same manner. She called out his name, and he responded by calling out her name. It was a perfect dance of two bodies, one taking the lead and the other following in perfect rhythm. Simple moves with a maximum of pleasure. Breaths competing with breaths, hands competing with hands, mouths competing with mouths, and all the while, Loraine was floating high on a cloud of wonder and surprise at every turn of the game.

And then she was lying peacefully in his arms. Her body relaxed, completely sated, and his hand was stroking her hair. His smile stretched across his face as though he could not make it big enough, and she could hear the steady beating of his heart as she lay with her head on his chest.

"Does this change our friendship status?" he asked.

"What sort of status were you looking for?" she asked back.

"Something as permanent as good friends, but goes a little deeper than, merely friends."

"Something like Loraine of the past and her lover had?"

"Hmmm, something like that. I think she really loved that man!"

"I don't know if I love you, Lawrence. I do like being with you though."

"Likewise, there is no rush for deep confessions, just contented comfortableness, is what I am looking for."

"I feel very comfortable right now."

"Me too. I could stay like this all night."

"My Aunt would wonder what had happened to you."

"Oh, she probably knows where I am. Give me the word, and we could do it all over again."

"I don't think that would be wise," she laughed. "It might turn into something more serious, and I don't think I'm ready for that yet."

"Yeah," he said softly. "We wouldn't want anything to get serious," He paused and looked at her. "Loraine, I think you are the best thing that has ever happened to me in a long time," He tilted her head up and kissed her. "I want this feeling to last forever."

"I am thinking that if people keep getting reincarnated, and meeting each other in future lives, those kinds of feelings *could* last forever."

"Do you think you will meet your past lover in this life, Loraine?" He started to feel a little worried about the possibility that she would, and then completely forget about him.

"I don't know who he is. I wouldn't know him, if I tripped over him."

"Well you have tripped over me, and I hope that will do for you."

"It may, it may," she breathed softly against his chest, and snuggled closer.

CHAPTER ELEVEN

Loraine hated pulling Lawrence away from his work, when she decided to try and visit her past. Besides, if he was in the room, she may try to jump his bones again, as he put it. Touching was one thing, but when she was in the past, no telling what she would do when she was in his arms. She had never had a sexual encounter with a man, other than Lawrence. She was glad he was the first. It had been a very fulfilling experience. But beyond that, she didn't like to think about her future relationship with Lawrence, because that meant she would have to analyze her feelings about him, and she wasn't ready for that, so she was just going to take it as it came, and then decide how she felt.

For now, she was anxious to learn about her 'other self', for she was sure that was who Amelia's mother was. Everything so far pointed to it. Her feelings about it all kept getting stronger, each time she learned some little new thing about what happened in the past, and there were times she actually thought she remembered things from the past, without going back in time through wearing the other Loraine's clothes.

What seemed so unrealistic though, was the fact that she not only looked like that other woman, but she had her name. That was too much of a coincidence. What were the odds that would really happen? She knew she was not related to the Landons on any level. If she was, she was totally unaware of it. So she came to the conclusion that reincarnation did not always stick with the same family, even though through the books she read on it, the same people seemed to come back together to work out karma with each other, either good or bad. But their relationships varied. So all of these people around her, must have some relationship to her in a past life, she reasoned.

It made her wonder about her crush on her cousin, and her feelings for Lawrence, as well. And then there was that fear of getting involved with men that kept plaguing her. Why would she feel that way? She had had a lover in the past, and the way she was always coming on to Lawrence when she strangely flipped into the past, just by looking into his eyes, indicated that she had enjoyed that relationship. It must have had something to do with Billings, she decided.

She unlocked the room, and went in, locking the door behind her. She was not worried about getting stuck in the past now, like she had before. She was not worried about getting stuck somewhere else when she came back to this time again. She knew she would come back to her own body in this room, and that her time traveling was really all in her head. A trigger of an old memory that she couldn't have any other way but through the effect that Loraine's old clothes had on her. She picked up the Album.

The photograph was taken of her on the front steps of the house. It was taken several months after the one with the banker. In fact, almost a year had passed since that picture had been taken, and the shoe factory had caught on fire, and the business was starting to fail, yet she looked happy in that photograph. When she looked at it, her heart seemed to lift up, and she could tell that Loraine of the past was unusually content in that photograph.

She couldn't tell the color of the dress, since the photos were in black and white, so she had to go by the style and cut of the gown, in order to find the same one in the wardrobe. This dress was easy to find, because it was fashioned like a sailor suit, with the square collar, most likely trimmed in blue stripes, and the dress looked like it was white. The sleeves at the shoulders were long puffs to the elbow, and then the rest of the sleeve fit tight against her arm to her wrist, where another double row of stripes were sewn. The hem of the dress, reaching almost to her ankles, had three thin dark stripes, and she wore white button up short top boots. A parasol, still folded, was held against the step in one gloved hand, like a cane, and it too was white with stripes around the edges. Loraine loved that picture.

She went to the wardrobe and pulled out the dress, almost finding it immediately, since it was not like any of the other dresses there. She wondered where the parasol was, but that was not important. As soon as she put on the dress, all other things seemed to materialize, and she realized that was because it was all in her mind, that she traveled in time, like a living dream because it seemed so real to her.

She was dressed, and was just pulling her gloves on, when she heard her mother calling to her through her door. Loraine opened the door, and stepped into the hall, looking over the banister into the entry below.

"Come down here and meet your cousin, Loraine. He has just arrived, with his sister from New York."

Loraine raised her eyebrows. She didn't even know they had any relatives in New York. But then she remembered that there had to be relatives in New York, because the other end of the business was there. The family just never talked about them. How exciting to have cousins!

She hurried down the stairs, and into the front parlor, just as her mother entered the room ahead of her. Loraine stood in the doorway, glancing over the room. Her father was there, looking a little grim, talking quietly to a young man who had his back to her. There was a lovely, dark headed woman sitting primly on the settee, dressed in a soft blue raised polka dot dress, with ruffles at the hem. She looked a little frightened.

Then Loraine entered the room, the young man turned and

looked at her. Loraine took in her breath. It was Lawrence standing there, and a chill went through her, because she recognized this man, who had not said a word to her yet. This…cousin…with the dark hair, and dark eyes, that penetrated her soul, just the same way Lawrence's eyes did. She had not remembered his name, but she knew exactly what it was, before her father even introduced him to her.

"Loraine, dear, I would like you to meet your cousins. This is Ella, and her older brother, Lawrence. They have come all the way from New York to visit. Checking up on the business, really."

Her father seemed nervous. And Loraine could tell by the way he kept glancing at her, and then at Lawrence, that he did not like Lawrence very much, even though he didn't seem to have any concern about the girl.

Loraine reached out for the door-jam to steady herself. She knew at that moment, even though her cousin didn't know it, that this was Loraine's lover from the past. Her own cousin… and the double of Lawrence of the future. That was why he had affected her that way. She had remembered him from the past, and she couldn't remember his name, because they were both the same. 'Him' was the other name she had given Lawrence to keep them separate in her mind, because she knew instinctively that she had loved the Lawrence of the past, and it had nothing to do with the Lawrence of the present. Yet, they both looked like their past counterparts. That seemed significant. However, Lawrence of the future was actually related to the family, so no wonder he looked like Lawrence of the past, she reasoned.

"Are you all right, Loraine?" her mother was asking. Lawrence was looking at her strangely as well, and instinctively stepped forward, and put his hand out, as though to steady her, but realized the impropriety of the action by the time he reached her side, and merely offered her his hand in greeting, taking her gloved hand in his and lifting it lightly to his mouth, while giving a little bow. It was a formal greeting, but being related, he could get away with it.

"So pleased I can finally meet my cousin across the states," he mumbled, looking deeply into her eyes.

Loraine steadied herself, and swallowed hard. She hoped she did not lose control of herself and make a fool of herself in front of him, and her parents. "I was not aware I had any cousins," was all she said.

"We have never been mentioned? Yet my father has spoken of you many times, though we have never had the chance to meet."

"It is so very far away," she murmured.

"The business keeps in touch. Strange our families don't. I was sent here about the business, so now it has given me and my sister a great excuse to get acquainted with you. However, we were killing two birds with one stone. You see, my sister has been betrothed, and I was escorting her down here to join the man she is to marry. He owns a fleet of ships, and my sister, with the chaperone of his mother, of course, will be sailing with him, back to New York, in order to get acquainted on the return trip, before the wedding takes place. She had never met him, you see, and refused to marry him, unless she got to meet him and judge his character. So father said I should pop in and see why business was slowing down at this end of the company, while I was here."

"Will you be leaving with your sister?" she asked, thinking that their acquaintance would be brief, if that was the case.

"She will be leaving within the week. But unless my business is tied up by then, I will probably be staying on."

"Our daughter is betrothed as well," Lorain's father stepped in, giving Lawrence a stern look at the way he was being so friendly to Loraine.

Loraine frowned. She had pleaded against the marriage, and still he persisted, though the announcement had not been made yet. "Please, father. I have not agreed to this," she said under her breath.

Lawrence's face lifted. She had been attracted to him, the moment their eyes met, and the pull was so strong, she could barely breathe.

"Well, Lawrence, we have business to discuss, perhaps you can take Ella out for a walk, Loraine," he suggested.

"I would love too." She smiled deeply at the frightened girl, who was a little younger than herself, and Ella rose up from the settee and followed Loraine out the front door.

"Would you like to stroll along the beach?" she asked. "We have our own private beach, so we will not encounter anyone."

"I brought my camera to take photographs. It is the latest fad, having a camera," Ella smiled. "Let me take your picture so I can remember you. I'll send you a copy when I get it developed."

Lorain posed on the front step to let Ella take her picture, and then she took one of Ella in return.

"Shall we head to the beach? You can take some photographs there as well," Loraine suggested.

"That sounds nice," Ella answered in a soft voice.

The two waked out along the shore, as the ocean breeze snatched at their skirts, and threatened to ruin their hairdos. Ella stuffed her camera in her shoulder bag and tightened the ribbons of her bonnet, but Loraine had not worn anything on her head, and already the strands of her hair were weaving around her face.

"We live on the shore, in New York, as well," Ella offered. "The Ocean here seems much the same, except it is on the opposite side of the States."

"I assume it is warmer here, though," Loraine said, trying to make small talk.

"Yes, it *is* warmer here," but she gave a little shiver.

"Then why do you act like you are cold?" Loraine asked.

"I am not cold. I...I am merely apprehensive. Tomorrow I am supposed to meet the man I am to marry for the first time. I am told he is handsome, but I am afraid I may not like him, and how would I ever brake off, if that was the case? My family would disown me."

"I know how you feel. My father wants me to marry a man I *have* met, but I am repulsed by him. I have begged and pleaded, but he says I will never choose anyone myself, so he will have done with it, and make me marry Mr. Billings."

"Why are parents so bent on dictating the lives of their children?" Ella asked. "If I have children, I will let them make their own choices."

"Yes, I am feeling the same way. I don't know what I am going to do, but I refuse to marry Mr. Billings, even if I have to run away to escape him."

"Where would you go? A woman cannot make her way in this world on her own."

"I know. But I would rather die, than be faced with a future with that repulsive man."

"Maybe my brother could help you," Ella suggested, with a cheery smile.

"I could not lay my burdens on him," Loraine murmured,

but wishing there was something her cousin could do to save her from a fate beyond her control.

"Still, we are family. We should help each other out," Ella persisted.

"What could your brother do? He is not responsible for me."

Ella wrinkled her nose, and shrugged. "I don't know, but we will talk to him, and speaking of him, there he is now, coming towards us!"

She turned and ran back up the beach to meet her brother half way, but Loraine held her ground. She was going to have to talk to him now, and the maddening undercurrents that were pulling at her heart, would certainly get in the way.

Lawrence smiled broadly at her, when he arrived before her, but strangely, he did not have a dimple like Lawrence of the present. Because of this discovery, she was staring at his cheek, and he lifted his eyebrow.

"Do I have something on my face?" he asked, reaching his gloved hand to the place on his cheek she was staring at.

"No...no, nothing at all," Loraine said, which was the truth... not even a dimple, she thought.

"Our business ended sooner than I expected, so I asked permission to join the two of you out here," he explained. "I so want to get to know you better."

Loraine thought to herself how *much* better Lawrence was about to get to know her, and smiled to herself.

"I feel the same way," she admitted, as she placed her hand on his arm and Ella took the other arm, as they continued to walk along the shore.

Loraine stopped and sat in the sand, tugging off her gloves and putting them in her pocket, and then began to remove her shoes. She pulled her stockings off and put them inside her boots. Ella raised her eyebrows, and Lawrence merely laughed.

"You can't walk on the beach without feeling the sand between your toes," Loraine offered.

"Certainly not!" Lawrence answered, and he pulled his gloves off as well, and sat down beside her to remove his shoes too. "Come on, Ella, be daring and take your shoes off."

Ella looked hesitant, but then slowly joined the two and pulled her shoes and stockings off the same as them, knowing it was very improper, but wanting to live dangerously.

"We'll leave our shoes here, and pick them up on our way back," he suggested, as he stood up and brushed the sand off the back of his pants. Then seeing sand clinging to Loraine's dress, he began to brush that off too. The feel of his hand, against her bottom, even with three petticoats to buffer it, caused Loraine's heart to speed, and she hoped he did not notice the warm glow that was spreading over her face.

Lawrence rolled up his slacks, and grabbed the girl's hands. "With our shoes abandoned, we must take advantage of the ocean, and not only feel the sand between our toes, but the salt water, splashing about our ankles," he insisted, and he pulled the girls with him as he jogged along the surf, that was rolling onto the sand.

The hem of Loraine's dress was getting wet, but she didn't care. The feel of the wind in her face, and the spray against her bare ankles, and the tightness of Lawrence's grip on her hand, was all she was thinking of at the time.

"I love people who are good sports," he told Loraine, as they slowed their pace, and walked in the surf. A wave sprayed up higher than expected, and Loraine lifted her skirt to her knees to prevent it from getting soaked more than it already was.

Lawrence admired her bare legs, as she scampered up ahead of him, her skirts lifted to her knees, and her hair half falling from its pins.

"She's a beautiful girl," Ella said at his shoulder. I can see you like her."

"Yes, she is beautiful... very beautiful."

"And her father is going to force her to marry some ogre, whom she hates. She says she would rather run away or die before she would marry him."

"Is that so? What a cruel world this is." Lawrence's eyes

turned dark, and his brow furrowed.

"You can help her, Lawrence. Use that brain of yours and think of something," his sister prompted.

"The only way I could keep her from marrying someone, is to offer for her myself, and that is highly unlikely, seeing as how we just met, and we are cousins."

"Cousins can marry. They do it in England all the time," Ella reasoned, sweetly.

"So they do. But would she want to marry her cousin? She may think she would be jumping out of the frying pan into the fire," he warned.

"Why don't you ask her, and find out?"

"On our first meeting? You are joking of course."

"There isn't much time. It should be settled before you are ready to return to New York. And after all, I am about to marry someone I have never seen, so what does that have to do with anything?"

"What if her father refuses to let me? He doesn't seem to like me much."

"Then you will have to elope," she suggested.

"Seems like you have this all figured out, little sister. You are not only ordering my life, but you are ordering hers. What makes you think I want to marry her anyway?"

"By the way you have been looking at her from the

moment she walked into that room! I am going to go over and sit on that rock, to rest, and you are going to catch up with her, and present the solution to her problem."

He shook his head, and she gave him a little push. "Go on! I will be waiting right here. There is a bend around that outcrop of rocks, and you can find some privacy there."

"Little match maker you are turning out to be. Or is it just a protecting angel, trying to solve the world's cruelties all on her own?" Lawrence winked, and patted her hand.

She pulled her hand back, waved him away, then went over and sat on the rock, taking her camera out to take more pictures while she waited. She pointed the camera at him and snapped one of him walking away.

It didn't take Lawrence long to catch up with Loraine, and he grabbed her hand and pulled her with him, as he sprinted forward. "Little sister wants to rest a bit, and she has told me some very disturbing things about you."

Loraine looked up at him. "Is that so? What did she say?"

"She told me about your pending marriage to some ogre, and how she insists that I help you out of a tight spot." He was pulling her slowly to the rocks.

"You are not required to help me," Loraine said, feeling nervous.

"Oh, but I am. I want to help you. I insist that you allow

me to help you." He looked at her with pleading eyes.

"What could you ever do?" she asked, wide eyed.

They were in the shelter of the rocks now and he bent his head closer to hers. "Marry you myself," he said simply.

Loraine's head jerked up. "Why, that is absurd! I don't even know you, and we are cousins," she pointed out.

"It's either me or the ogre," he said with a coaxing smile. "If there was any other solution, I would offer it, but I fear that is the only remedy I can think of. The truth is, I would most welcome it, because I feel as though I have known you all my life. The moment you walked into the room, I felt my heart swell, with my attraction to you. The only question now, is, are you as attracted to me?" He looked closely into her eyes.

"I...I hadn't thought, about it, but I have to admit, I am very much attracted to you," Loraine blushed, "Yet marrying you, never crossed my mind."

"I believe you would if I offered, which I have, so please say yes," Lawrence stated, and as she opened her mouth in shock at his insistence, he placed his mouth over hers, silencing any objections she may have, and crushing her in his arms. "Say, yes, and your problem will be solved," he whispered, as their lips parted.

"Are you sure you wish this?" Loraine questioned, feeling a little unsure of herself, but the draw was so strong, and the way his lips had felt on hers, was already making her mind up for her.

"I wish it, more than you know," Lawrence admitted, and he was pulling her to the sand, as his mouth found hers again, and his kiss deepened, causing Loraine to forget that she had just met this cousin. It seemed right being in his arms, with his mouth doing wonderful things to her senses.

Her arms were about his neck, pulling herself tightly against him. When they broke apart, she was breathless, and she shook her head, causing the rest of her hair to fall around her shoulders.

"Father, would never allow it! And...and you don't even know me. And...and I ...I don't think they allow cousins to marry in America!"

"None of those reasons will deter me," he told her. "The moment I saw you, I knew you were the only woman for me. If your father refuses, we will elope. There will be nothing he can do about it."

"If he knows you want to marry me, he will lock me in my room until you leave. Don't ask him. Don't tell him. He will send you away if he even thought you might like me a little!"

"Then we will have to make some subtle plans, but in the meantime, I have to discover why your father's business is going under, and why the orders are not making it out to the shops. That will give us more time to arrange things between us."

"Good." Loraine breathed, not believing her good fortune that her cousin showed up when he did, and then fell in love with her instantly. She felt she had fallen in love with him instantly as well, and she was so happy, she could hardly contain her joy.

Lawrence filled his fingers with her long golden hair, and pulled her head back, penetrating her green emerald eyes with his obsidian ones. Fire seemed to leap between their eyes, and passion raised in their breasts. To quench the need of her, he grabbed her to him and attacked her mouth with a frenzy of desire, his hand caressing her bare leg, pushed up under her skirt to her waist, and Loraine was reminded of another Lawrence, and another beach, but the feelings were still the same, strong and overpowering, as she felt his hand touching her at the opening of her pantalets, pushing for access that would promise a wonderful reward, and she was not going to stop him.

The wild caresses did not last long, because Ella was waiting for them, and Loraine pulled her hair back up, as well as she could, and replaced the pins, but her face was aglow, and her lips were bruised by his kisses, and her heart was still thudding rapidly in her chest, and her soul sang out for joy because she would be saved from a fate worse than death, and rescued by a handsome angel, who wanted her more than life itself. Or so he told her.

Loraine returned to her room, when they reached the house.

Ella had been so pleased when Lawrence told her of their plans. Loraine's face was still flushed, and she was so rumpled, that she was glad they did not encounter her parents when they came through the entry. She raced up the stairs, and as soon as the door was closed, she removed her damp, sandy dress, and everything was back to normal again.

Lorain was sitting in the pink room, in her own time period, but her heart was still racing, and she thought she could still feel Lawrence's kiss upon her lips, and she touched them, as she realized that Lawrence, of the past, looking like Lawrence of the present, except for the dimple, had been her lover. Was he and Lawrence of the present the same soul, reincarnated? Was that why his eyes caused her to flip back into the past?

Then she thought of Randy. He was her real cousin, and that must be why she was drawn to him so much. She had somehow subtly remembered that she was in love with her cousin in the past, and thought of Randy as that cousin. Only when she had kissed him, she realized he was not the one, and she couldn't understand it.

What was she ever going to tell Lawrence, she wondered? Should she tell him? It just might complicate everything if she did. No. Lawrence should not find out, she decided. Not yet, anyway.

CHAPTER TWELVE

Loraine did not tell Lawrence that she had traveled back in time, while he was not with her. She was afraid she would tell him about her cousin, and he would want to know more about it. He knew that the cousin's name was Lawrence, because he had been named after that distant relative. He knew that the cousin had disappeared, and that Loraine's father had claimed that he had left, shortly after his sister did, but he had never returned home. She needed to find out what Mr. Billings had to do with all of this. If he learned of her love affair with her cousin, maybe he was the cause of Lawrence's disappearance. She had to find out more about Mr. Billings, but she was not sure how she was going to go about doing that. If she could find the diary...she decided to search for it, to occupy her time, and tell Lawrence that was why she had not gone back to the past again, if he asked, because she was spending her time looking for the diary. Also, now that she had learned who Lawrence was, she was almost afraid to go back to the past again.

She decided a complete search of the room was the only way she would find the book, if there was a book, so she started her search in the box of books, which seemed too obvious, and it turned up nothing. She looked in the trunk of clothes, and still turned up nothing. She searched in the wardrobe, in all the hat boxes, in the box of dolls, and still, no book. Maybe there wasn't a book. Maybe Loraine did not write any of this down. Maybe she should go back in time to find out if Loraine did keep a diary, and where she may have put it. Only the risk of going back in time was too great for her at the moment. Everything was too fresh in her mind, concerning her feelings for that cousin of the past, and she wanted to give herself time to let her emotions settle down.

She would spend time with Amelia, she decided. They had almost abandoned her, what with Lawrence working on the yard that was shaping up so nicely, and her spending so much time in the locked room, looking for answers and living in the past. She would dedicate a whole day to being with the old woman, and keeping her company.

Loraine found Amelia in the parlor, puttering with her doll house. "That stupid old woman," she was muttering.

"Hello," Loraine interrupted her. "Why are you so upset?" She could see the scowl on Amelia's face.

"That old housekeeper enjoys making my life miserable. She knows I can't get rid of her, and she keeps doing little things to irritate me."

"What has she done that has upset you today?" She gave Amelia a sympathetic look.

"She took my box of material that I use to work on my doll house with. Said she thought it was trash, and took it up to the attic. She knew what it was, and she knows I can't get up there to get it."

"Why would she stop you from working on the doll house?" Loraine questioned, thinking the housekeeper was over stepping her bounds, and someone should give her a good talking to.

"Just to irritate me. She is as bad as my Grandfather was. She knows I am helpless, and she is just mean spirited and likes to see me get in a dither, and then gloats because I can't do anything about it. Since you came, it has gotten worse, because she knows I am happy having you here, and she wants me to stay as miserable as I was when my Grandfather was alive."

"That is horrible. I am sure if you speak to the solicitors they will allow you to remove her from your home, in spite of the will."

"Perhaps, but she knows the house so well, after all these years. How would I replace her? She knows I need her here and gloats over the fact."

"Then, how can *I* help you?"

"You can go to the attic, and look for my box of odds and ends, and bring them back to me. I will keep them hidden so she can't take them away again," Amelia suggested.

"How do I get to the attic? I have never been up there before."

"Use the back stairs, from the kitchen. Just make sure Mary doesn't see you."

Loraine started out towards the kitchen, but as she was passing though, she saw Lawrence getting a drink of water.

"Hey there, beautiful," he called. Where have you been keeping yourself lately? I hardly ever see you anymore." He came up closer to her. "I thought we were going to be more than just friends, and you have been keeping your distance, ever since that night spent in the locked room." He gave her a little disappointed frown.

He was right. She was starting to feel panicky again, and now more than ever, since she found out who Lawrence was in the past. He would take it all too personally, if he knew. "I have been looking for the diary and have turned the room upside down trying to find it," she told him truthfully.

"And it hasn't turned up?"

"No, I'm afraid not."

"So, you still have the dresses you can use to jog your memory. The diary would just confirm everything you already know anyway, if it exists," he pointed out.

"I just want to find it because I don't know that much about the banker yet, and how am I going to find out what dress she wears when or if she sees him again?'

"Well then, keep looking. You might end up finding it. Probably some place you least expect to."

"Yeah, it is always in the last place that you look," she laughed.

"Where are you off to now?"

"To the attic, I have to find a box of stuff that the housekeeper took from Amelia and stuck in there, so she couldn't get to it. The lady is positively mean."

"Want any help?" Lawrence offered.

"Yeah, I could use some help, since I have no idea where she stuck the box, or what it looks like, but it is probably the one that has the least amount of dust collected on it, I am sure," Loraine laughed.

Loraine started up the back stairs, and Lawrence followed her. The attic was huge. It spanned the entire floor plan of the house, which was nothing to blink at. And there were boxes and trunks, old furniture, appliances, picture frames, with and without paintings in them, lamps, both modern and ancient. They saw old rolls of wallpaper, probably for back up repairs of the wall paper already on the walls. There were so many things Loraine didn't know where to start. Yet at the same time, everything looked exciting to her, because this room held the history of the house, that was somewhat hidden from view.

"Everything looks pretty dusty to me," Lawrence commented, as he swiped a finger across the closest box to him.

"The housekeeper probably knew we wouldn't be able to find that box, even if Amelia told us about her taking it." Loraine admitted, but determined not to give up right away.

"You take that end of the attic, and I will take this end, and whoever finds it first, let out a yell," Lawrence suggested, taking the bull by the horns.

Loraine looked around her, bewilderedly. "How are we ever going to find anything in this mess, unless we know right where she put it?'

"Just keep looking. You don't want to disappoint Amelia, do you?" Lawrence, himself was finding this place intriguing. There must be a goldmine worth of old things up here, he thought. "Look at this old suitcase," he said. "They don't make them like that anymore. Straps around them to hold them shut, and so heavy, once you put your clothes in them, you can barely pick them up!" He demonstrated by lifting the dusty old suitcase up. "Feels like it is *still* full of stuff," he said.

"Will you stop messing around?" Loraine scolded.

"Why take all the fun out of the job? Now I'm wondering what is in that old suitcase," Lawrence stated, taking a closer look at the tattered looking piece of luggage.

"If it is going to drive you crazy, open it up and find out.

But I might remind you, we are looking for a box, not a suitcase."

Lawrence wasn't listening, because he was unbuckling the straps of the suitcase, and pushing the latch open. "Just some old clothes," he laughed, "And some spiffy looking clothes, at that, if I do say so myself! They even look like my size! He held up a pair of slacks to his waist."

Loraine turned from what she was doing, and glanced at Lawrence. He was in the process of putting his arms through the sleeves of on old shirt, and pulling on some grey gloves. She took in her breath, and practically ran over to his side, staring at him.

"What's the matter? You look like you have seen a ghost!" he said in astonishment.

"I think I have seen a ghost! Those clothes belong to Loraine's cousin from the past, the one who disappeared!"

"Really, how do you know?" He narrowed his eyes at her. "You went back again, didn't you? And without me being there!"

"It was perfectly safe. And nothing happened, but I met the cousin, and his sister, and he was wearing that outfit out on the beach, on the first day he came there!"

"So, apparently, he did not leave shortly after his sister, or maybe he did, but not with his belongings in tow." Lawrance started pulling things from the case. "There are quite a bit of things in here. If he left on his own, he would have taken his clothes with him!" Lawrence reasoned. As he spoke, he looked at

Loraine with widened eyes.

"What is it?" she asked, coming closer to him.

"I have his shirt on. The shirt he was wearing on the beach. You were wearing a cute little sailor outfit, and you had taken off your shoes and stockings, and...and," he grabbed her arm, "I'm kissing you! I'm holding you! God, it is the scene on the beach all over again, but it is in the past. Loraine, I can see it as clear as day! What is going on?"

Loraine shook, as Lawrence grabbed her other arm and looked into her eyes, and his head bent down, kissing her in the same way Lawrence had kissed her on the beach that day in her past.

"I wanted to marry you," he breathed, "and you loved me, as I loved you...I...I am the lover of your past, aren't I Loraine?"

She didn't say anything. She was afraid to say anything.

"And something happened to him. I can feel it. Something horrible happened to him!"

"Shh...shh..." she put her hand over his mouth. "Don't say that! Don't tell me that!"

"These are his clothes! These were my clothes. He never left this place... that we can be sure of."

"I...I don't know what happened to him. I...I just met him, that last time I went back..."

"And you didn't tell me? You kept it from me?"

"I...I was afraid! I didn't want you to..."

"Some friend, and sometime lover you are turning out to be," he stormed. "I was the one. I was the one all along, and when you looked at me, you knew! You knew, and yet you played coy, and hard to get, and acted like you didn't' want to get close to me. We are soul mates, for Christ sake, Loraine! And you...you shrugged it off like it meant nothing to you!"

Tears were quietly rolling down Loraine's face, and she didn't know how to explain it. "I...I didn't really know at first...I..."

"Like heck you didn't! You were jumping my bones, every time I turned around, and you couldn't feel it? That's a bunch of crock! It's that stupid fear you have of men, and you have lumped me into that definition of men you have drummed up to protect your poor little heart. No worry about my heart though, huh Loraine?"

"Don't say that..."

"Or...or maybe I was wrong. Maybe we are not soul mates. Not any more, anyway!"

He started ripping the shirt off his back, and tearing the gloves from his hands.

"I have had enough of this playacting, pretending to be lovers in the past, and yet not being honest with each other in the here and now. You have just been playing me, so you could find out more about the woman who has ruined your life in the future, because she couldn't handle anything in the past, and killed herself over it! Are you going to kill yourself too, Loraine? Are you?"

"No...NO!" she screamed. "How can you say that? I am trying to find out why *she* killed herself!"

"Without asking for my help, I might add! Yes, of course! This is your little drama, your little 'Miss Nancy Drew' mystery to figure out, and the starring role, is little Miss Loraine, forget about the hero, who disappears in the end. And that is what I am going to do, right about now. Disappear!"

He turned, and stocked down the stairs, without a backwards glance, leaving Loraine, drenched in tears, holding his shirt to her face, remembering what it felt like to have Lawrence hold her back then, and then shocked, as she realized that she was also remembering how Lawrence had held her just the other night, and touched her body the way he had, and now he would probably never speak to her again.

Loraine sank down to the floor, crying into the shirt. The shirt he had worn on that wonderful day on the beach. And something had happened to him, and she would never discover what it was. She knew her suicide had something to do with it, but none of the memories would come! She was holding them at bay. She didn't want to know what happened to him, and why it happened to him. She felt guilty. It was her fault! She knew it was her fault. And her father's! Anger surged through her. That was a secret her father had kept! That 'truth' she had mentioned in the suicide note. It was something he had never told Amelia either!

And now Lawrence hated her. Like her father of the past, she had kept the truth from him as well. She deserved it! It was her own fault. Besides, her love affair with Lawrence of the past must have turned out all wrong, because he had disappeared, and she had been left behind. Maybe he left on purpose. Maybe because she had done something to upset him, he had left without packing any of his clothes, just leaving them behind. Maybe he dashed off, just like Lawrence did just a few minutes ago, and something must have happened to him. But what, was this a sample of life repeating itself from the past?

If he had left on his own, her father would not have put his suitcase in the attic. He would have told his brother that his nephew had taken off and left his things behind. There would have been an investigation into his disappearance, she was sure. She started shaking. Her father had something to do with this, because the suitcase was hidden in the attic, and she had accused her father in her suicide note. Because of him, she was deprived of her happiness, and life had not been worth living, even with a brand new daughter to care for.

Loraine tried to pull herself together. She had lost interest in looking for the box for Amelia, and went slowly down stairs. She needed to go out and find Lawrence, and try to explain it all to him. If he would only listen… she went out to the garden, but she couldn't find him, and then she noticed his car was gone. It wasn't even noon yet, and he had taken off. He was angry. He probably went somewhere to cool off.

Loraine went back into the house, and found Amelia. "I'm sorry I couldn't find your box," she told her. "I will try looking again, but the attic is so big, it might take me awhile to locate it."

Amelia just nodded, blankly, which troubled Loraine.

"Did you and Lawrence have a fight?" she asked outright.

"Sort of," Loraine admitted.

"It must have been more than just a sort of fight. He told me he was going back to New York. He said something came up unexpectedly."

"Oh no, it's my fault. I didn't mean to make him so angry!" Loraine cried, her heart suddenly sinking, when she realized she may never see Lawrence again, just like herself of the past had never seen him again. He had told her he was going to disappear, and it was all her fault.

"Maybe you had better go after him before he leaves. He looked fit to be tied."

Loraine didn't stop to listen. She was already out the door and dashing to her car, putting the little bug in gear, and backing out of the driveway.

She screeched to a stop in front of her aunt's house, jumping out of the car, and not even bothering to close the door as she hurried to the back door, only to run smack dab into Randy.

"Hey there, little cousin..." he took one look at her face. "Oooo, I can tell this is not good! Lawrence just took out of here pell-mell, calling you pretty nasty names, I might add, and said he was heading home, never should have come in the first place, didn't want to talk about it, nice to meet you but good-bye, so long, fare well...etc, etc, etc."

"The pig-headed, self-centered, goof ball!" Loraine spat, "Doesn't give me a chance to explain anything! Just starts assuming...Oh! I have never met anyone who....who..." She was at a loss for words. "Who, I love so much, who I loved so much in the past, and who will never love me again!" She started to sob.

Randy put his arms around her. "Uh, I don't think I am following you. I know that guy was mad about you, but according to him you wouldn't have much to do with him."

"You know how relationships scare me. He was pushing too hard, and just when we were starting to get to know each other better, he flies off the handle because I wouldn't tell him about, him being my lover in the past."

"Okay...I thought you just met him. How can he be your lover in the past, without him knowing it?"

She gave Randy a helpless look. "It is a very long story, which I don't think you are going to believe. Do you think his plane has taken off yet?"

"He's not taking a plane. He says he's driving, it will give him time to think, he claims."

"Then I guess there is no way to stop him. I guess that is that." Loraine's shoulders slumped in resignation.

"In that case, you will have plenty of time to tell me the story," Randy told her. "And believe me, I will try to believe you. Just take it a step at a time." He led her back into the house and up to her old room, which Lawrence had vacated. "If you want your old room back, I guess it is available," he said softly.

"No, I have a much more interesting room than this. And it is what has started all the trouble in the first place."

Loraine began explaining to Randy everything that happened since she saw the old house on the hill as a child... the house that was taking her back to the past, and screwing up her here and now. Randy listened patiently, trying not to show his shock at places that were almost too hard to believe. But, apparently, she and Lawrence believed it was true, and that must be what was causing the whole misunderstanding between them.

"Now let me get this straight. You had a crush on me because I am your cousin, and in your past life you had loved your cousin, so it seemed natural to love your cousin again. But then, when I kissed you, you realized I was not your lover of the past? Are you trying to tell me that I am a lousy kisser, and Lawrence is better than me?" He gave Loraine a penetrating look, with a mock frown on his face.

Loraine laughed. "You are just trying to make me feel bad. You are a great kisser."

"And, don't forget, I also liked you a little bit, or I wouldn't have been trying to kiss you in the first place. So does that mean that in some past life we were lovers as well, but not the mad lovers you and Lawrence seemed to have been?"

"Oh, how do I know? I didn't even know anything about past lives, until all of this started to happen. But there must be some reason why I fear relationships. If Lawrence, of my past, just disappeared out of my life, it must have been devastating to me. Maybe I don't trust men because I was so hurt by his leaving me like that. After all, I threw over Billings, and jilted him at the altar. Can you imagine how angry Billings would have been? And then after all that, Lawrence just takes off. The baby she was carrying had to be his. I can't imagine her making love with Billings, unless he forced her, and when she was about to marry him, it was Lawrence she wanted to run off with. He had planned to marry her, to keep Billings from doing it. So why did he just take off?" Loraine gave a little shiver, as she thought about it.

"Maybe he didn't take off. Maybe Billings found out about

him planning to marry her. After all, he hadn't married her, since she was all dressed in her wedding dress, about to marry Billings. If he was going to marry her, to save her from Billings, she wouldn't be putting that wedding dress on. Maybe Billings did something to him, which gave Loraine no other choice but to marry Billings, and that is why Lawrence disappeared, without taking any of his clothes."

"But I don't think he disappeared yet, on the day of her wedding, because she was going to go out the window to run away with him. If Billings did away with him, then why would her father put the suitcase in the attic, and say Lawrence left shortly after his sister left?" she questioned.

"Maybe they were in it together, since he wanted her to marry Billings so much. Why did he want her to marry Billings? Do you know?"

"It had to have something to do with all the money he was borrowing from the bank. Maybe by her marrying Billings, and Billings being brought into the business as her husband, that would help the company out. Billings was loaded. She was his only daughter, and would inherit the business, once her father died, and maybe her father wanted to insure the company would continue running, not only after he died, but up to that point, as well."

"Yeah, and if Lawrence was going to marry her instead, it would mean that the two businesses, the one in New York, and one here in California, would merge as one, and her father did not seem to like Lawrence or his own brother. Remember, Lawrence said the family never kept in contact, except through the business. There had to be a reason for that."

"Why would the Landon brothers hate each other?" This was all looking a little complicated, and Loraine wondered if she was ever going to get to the bottom of it?

"Maybe it was just one sided. After all, Lawrence said that his father had told him about Loraine, but her father never spoke about the New York cousins," Randy offered.

"Yes, I could tell that Loraine's father did not like Lawrence, though he didn't seem to hate the girl in the same way." She paused, remembering the look her father of the past had given Lawrence, before he introduced them, and then made sure Lawrence knew she was promised to someone else, because he could tell the way Lawrence was looking at Loraine, meant something.

"Of course, he didn't like the son. It was the son that was falling all over Loraine, and her father informed him she was betrothed, even when she wasn't. He wanted to keep the man away from Loraine for some reason." Randy reasoned.

"Because it would screw up the wedding he had planned between her and Billings, which he needed to happen in order to save the business." Loraine surmised. "Only at that time nothing was solid. Loraine had refused to marry Billings, and told her father as much."

"But the other question is why was the business failing? It had been so successful before the fire, and the business in New York was doing well. How were the orders getting lost? That is where I think foul play has something to do with it, and I bet Billings was behind it." Randy wrinkled his forehead, as he tried to figure it out.

"If her father knew that, then he would never allow her to marry the man," Loraine insisted. "I wonder if he *did* know it and maybe Billings had something to hold over his head?"

"Which brings us back to Lawrence, and why he disappeared. Billings had to have had a hand in it," Randy was sure.

"She was going to climb out the window and meet him. I wonder if she ever did?" Loraine almost murmured to herself.

"Maybe you should go back and see," Randy encouraged.

"Not yet, not yet. It would be too painful right now. I know she never got together with him. But maybe I will try and find out if Billings was interfering with the orders in some way."

"Seems the only answer to all of this," Randy agreed.

"And I think I have some explaining to do to Amelia, too. I have been keeping the truth from her, just like I was keeping it from Lawrence, and apparently holding back the truth in the past was what ruined Loraine's life back then. Maybe I should just be up front, and hope the information doesn't kill her.

"I learned, while reading about reincarnation, that the reason people keep coming back is to repair the mistakes of their past lives, and if they have bad karma to work out, they need to fix it, and if they have good karma, they will meet those people and enjoy the same loving relationship they had with them in the past.

"Loraine left her infant daughter behind, with no mother to love her, and a terrible grandfather to raise her. I think that is the karma I need to work out with Amelia. I don't know what kind of karma I need to work out with Lawrence though. If he left Loraine back then maybe he is the one who needs to work it out with me. But it will have to be his choice, not mine."

"Then just take care of your karma with Amelia, and let the rest work itself out. Just break it to her gently. She wanted to find out before she died anyway," Randy soothed.

"I wished I could find Loraine's diary, if she kept one. It would be easier than going back in time."

"Face it, Loraine, you enjoy experiencing that past life, and you feel it more personally that way. Had you just found the diary, you wouldn't realize that you were Loraine of the past, and you would have missed all this drama involved in that life."

"All this drama is going to be the death of me," Loraine sighed.

Randy put his arm around his cousin's shoulder. "Lawrence left me his phone number in New York. After we find out all the answers, maybe we should call him, and see if he changes his mind about you," Randy said, trying to cheer Loraine up.

Loraine shook her head. "He'll never speak to me again. You should have seen the way he looked at me when he discovered that I knew we were supposedly soul mates, and I didn't tell him about it, it must have really hurt him to think I didn't trust him enough to tell him. And he was right. I didn't only not trust him, but I didn't trust myself. I was afraid, Randy. I was afraid to let my heart love him the same way it did back then. That is probably why I shun all men. I am just afraid to love anyone anymore."

"Oh, he'll get over it. If he really loves you, he'll come back, and then you need to confess all."

"I guess I have really screwed everything up. I just don't know how to deal with men!" Loraine's voice shook, as she remembered the look on Lawrence's face, before he stormed from the attic.

"Tell me about it, little cousin. Tell me about it. I am always picking the wrong kind of women. Maybe in the back of my mind, I am waiting for someone like you to come along," he smiled, kissing her on the nose.

CHAPTER THIRTEEN

Loraine dreaded having to explain everything to Amelia, but it wasn't fair that she kept it from her any more. She decided to make one last ditch try in looking for the diary, before she had to face her. If she had the diary, maybe Amelia could read it all for herself.

She went into the locked room, but she had already searched that whole room. She went to the box of books. Maybe the diary was hidden inside some other book, like the keys were. She rummaged through the books, but discovered nothing. Absently, she picked up the book of poems by Keats, and it fell open at the poem that Lawrence had read to her. Now, the poem seemed to have so much more meaning to her, a lover coming back from the dead to speak words of love once more, or something to that affect. She never understood half of Keats' poetry.

She started to read it again, and as the words formed in her mind, she was transported back in time. She was in a cave on the beach. Lawrence was sitting on a blanket beside her in that cave, and he was reading Keats to her... that very poem. That is why it sounded so familiar to her when she first heard it. The words began to soak in, and she looked around the cave.

It wasn't very large, and she could see the waves crashing on the beach not far from the opening. It must be located somewhere on their own beach. She knew she had met him on the beach to be with him alone, and he had brought her to this cave. He must have just found it himself, since he was not familiar with the area.

She was lying with her head in his lap, as he read, and his voice resonated in her ears, but she wasn't listening so much to the words, as she was to the sound of his voice. She loved the sound of his voice.

Loraine, realized, she was not thinking this memory, she was there, as though she had put on one of Loraine's dresses, but she hadn't put on any of her dresses. She had just read the poem, and it transported her back in time the same way Loraine's clothes had. It was easier for her to flash back in time, now, she realized. Perhaps it was the room that was doing it to her, she thought.

"Are you paying attention, sweetheart?" he was asking, and she smiled up at him.

"To every word!" she told him. "I love listening to your voice."

His hand was absently stroking her hair as he read, but now he lay the book aside, and looked down into her sparkling green globs that overwhelmed him, every time he gazed at her. He brought her head up to him, and kissed her lips.

"We have to make plans, Loraine. There isn't much time, and your marriage has already been announced in the newspaper. You won't be able to hold your father off much longer."

"Can't we just leave?" she asked flinging her arms around his neck and holding him close to her.

"I would have to make arrangements, and we can't travel together alone, unless we are legally married. That is what is going to be tricky."

"Not if I pretended to be your sister," Loraine told him. "You came here with your sister, didn't you?"

"Yes. That may work. No one would know you weren't my sister."

"I can't wait to get away from this place, away from Mr. Billings and my father, who just won't listen to reason."

"I won't let that man marry you, Loraine. You belong to me." He kissed her with desperation, stroking her face with his hand, crushing her to him in a way he had never dreamed of cradling a woman before. As Loraine experienced this event of the past, it now seemed like she could read his every thought. She knew that every time he was with her, his senses went berserk, and all he could think of was holding her, and kissing her, and touching her. She would soon be his legally, but he wanted her to be his completely, wholeheartedly, intimately. The thought of Billings ever touching her with even one finger, drove him mad, and he wanted some way to make her permanently his, even before he ever managed to marry her. If she was completely his, Billings could never have her. Her father would have to allow her to marry him if she admitted to being compromised by him, and he knew she would do it willingly.

And it was that thought that encouraged him onward. His kisses became more demanding, and she responded to him eagerly. As he captured her mouth in his, he slowly and deliberately began to unfasten the buttons down the front of her pretty pink dress. She was too caught up in his kisses to realize what he was doing, or she wanted him to do it, she wasn't sure. But regardless of the reason, she welcomed everything that Lawrence was doing.

His skin burned for her, and his heart was pumping blood so fast through his veins, that his whole body felt like it was on fire. His arousal was already strong, and she was lying in his lap, the movement of her body stimulating him even more. He realized he had stopped calculating his actions. They seemed to come naturally.

The feel of her skin under his fingers, her bare, bare skin, as he pushed the top of her dress aside, lowering his head to ravish her with his mouth. And he felt her under his lips, the feel of her swallowing as his mouth kissed her neck, the lift of her breasts, as she took in a breath. Her little murmur, when she felt his tongue tasting her, his mouth holding her, his hands kneading her skin, where his mouth was not devouring her. And he knew he could have her. He could have every inch of her, and then she would be his for eternity.

His complete knowledge of that drove him on, as the top of her dress fell completely from her body, and she was there in all her enticing beauty, and adorableness, giving herself to him without his asking. Allowing him to kiss and fondle that body which he loved so much.

He wanted to feel that extraordinary body, next to his bare skin, and he removed his shirt, lowering himself down beside her, pulling her and her soft breasts against his strong hard chest, feeling them burn into his skin by their very touch, and his loins were exploding to have her, to feel warm within her, and make her his, and no one else's.

Her skirt and petticoats were not easy to maneuver, but when he finally had her down to her pantalets, the rest was easy, and that was the part that mattered the most, exploring her and. finding a place to let nature take its course.

She had her eyes closed. Probably feeling too embarrassed to look at him, or wanting to even know exactly what he was doing, but she could feel what he was doing, and he could tell she liked what he was doing, by the way she responded to him, with murmurs, sighs, and gasps of pleasure. And, yes, he wanted to pleasure her. To pleasure every part of her, leaving nothing untouched, or experienced. He wanted to experience her completely. He wanted her to experience him completely, and it was time to graduate to that next step, while she was breathing hard, and arching her lovely little back, and moaning in rapture, as if begging for him to have her with that part of his body that would make her his own, in just a few strokes, or however long it took, as he did not want to hurt her.

He heard her gasp, whether it was with surprise or shock, he wasn't sure, but his mouth smothered that gasp, and did not allow her to speak. At first her hands pushed hard against his chest, trying to wriggle free of him, but he swallowed her exclamations into his mouth, to smother her sudden fear, while he moved evenly, slowly, passionately, willing her body to respond. Then he slowly felt her relaxing, with each new movement, each new caress, each new found sensation, that started to bring her to him, welcomingly, wantonly, desperately, as their frenzy began to mount. The urgency began to demand, and the desire took and gave and gasped with wonder, as their union became a natural part of the dance, that started to whirl out of control.

Nothing could stop them now, as their breaths caught in unison, and their heart beats raced beyond limitation, climbing higher, trying to reach that plateau that could send them into the universe, into a million splintered pieces, spreading out and encompassing the unknown. Then it slowly allowed them to fall to earth again in tingling awareness, that they had become one, through that act. It felt like they had become a single person through their connection of body and souls, never separating that oneness, but welding it even tighter with each future act of coming together.

Lorain lay quietly in his arms, afraid to speak, afraid to move. He was still a part of her, and she wanted him to remain that way for as long as possible, though she didn't know how long that could be?

He said nothing, but nuzzled his face into her hair and stroked her back, trying to catch his breath at the discovery of how wonderful she felt in his arms, with him so immersed in the feel of it, he never wanted to part from her. He played absently with her long strands of hair, as he kissed her forehead, and then his hands smoothed down over her hip, that were pressed so snuggly against him. He felt himself wanting her again.

The mad need of her consumed him, even now, when he should be too tired to move, or to feel anything, but it was there, pushing now, wanting now, desiring more of her. Always more of her, and he turned her on her back, and began the sensual dance once again, feeling her begin to move to meet his desire, and they were lost together in time and space, reaching out for more completeness, for more oneness, for that effervescent fulfillment that only the two of them could create, as they struggled to remain as one.

When they finally relaxed, Lawrence knew she was his forever. She would always be his, to the day he died, and no man would ever touch her but himself, because they were bound by something stronger than life itself. They were bound by eternity.

Loraine gasped, as the memory slid away. She had felt it as though it had really happened, and she knew she was irrevocably tied to Lawrence, even today, and he *had* been her soul mate. He was still her soul mate! Something had prevented them from remaining together in the past, and now they had the opportunity to make it right in this life. He had to come back to her, she thought. He had to. She knew for certain then that Amelia was Lawrence's child as well as hers. She wondered if he ever discovered she was going to have his baby, back then.

That must be the reason he came here, just like she did, to make it up to Amelia, because they could never be her parents in the past. But what stopped them, she wondered? His disappearance was the reason. It had to be.

Loraine had not found the diary, but she had found some more answers, and she decided it was time to tell Amelia, and let the chips fall where they may, hoping against hope, that the frail woman could deal with the truth.

Loraine found Amelia in the parlor, staring forlornly at the doll house. She felt sorry for the woman...the old woman who was her daughter in the past, whom she had held only briefly, and then abandoned in death. She was Lawrence's daughter as well, and the story had to be told. She wondered if Amelia would believe her, if she told her, that she had been her mother in a past life? She could just say she was psychic, and knew that her mother's cousin was her father, and leave it at that. But that did not seem right. She had to risk it, she decided.

Amelia looked up into Loraine, eyes, and seemed to be aware of the pain there. "Did you find Lawrence? Did you stop him from going back to New York?"

"No, and he left because of me. I am sorry, because I know how much you enjoyed having him here."

"But I thought he liked you. I could tell he liked you, so what happened? You liked him too, didn't you?" Amelia's brow puckered in concern.

"Yes, I liked him very much. In fact you might say that I loved him, but now it might be too late to do anything about it."

"Oh, no. True love will always find a way," Amelia told her, firmly.

"I would like to believe that, but when you hear what I have to tell you, you might change your mind about that."

"I am listening," she said quietly, seeming to know that something serious was about to be revealed.

Loraine took a deep breath, and then plunged forward,

before she lost her nerve. "I have a confession to make," she started out slowly, trying to calculate her words. "Lawrence and I found the key to the locked room. It was hidden behind a brick in the back wall, and when Lawrence pulled the ivy off the house, it pulled the brick out with it."

Amelia gasped. "I guess it was a good thing I let him work on the yard," she commented.

"Yes, it was. I think his coming here, and my coming here was sort of like fate. You needed to find out about your past, and we needed to discover our connection to each other and our connection to you as well."

"I am not sure what you mean," Amelia's eyes looked puzzled.

"I will explain, but I want to tell you about the locked room. It looks just like the yellow room, but it is all done in pink, so it should be easy for you to duplicate it in the doll house. The furniture is a little different. If Lawrence was here I would have him carry you upstairs so you could see it, but for now, I will just tell you about it." Loraine continued to describe the room to Amelia, and then she jumped up. "I...I forgot! I found pictures of your mother. Paintings and her photograph album. I will go get them for you."

Loraine ran upstairs, and grabbed the paintings, and the album, returning to the parlor, out of breath. "Now, I don't want you to get freaked out, when you see these pictures, because I will explain it all to you. But it will make it easier to do so, if you see the pictures."

Amelia's brow drew together, but when Loraine turned the first painting, so Amelia could see it, she gasped, and her face looked a little shocked, and then very pleased.

"I knew it. I just knew it! When I heard you had my mother's name, I had to hire you, and then when you came here, I noticed you looked a little like me when I was a girl. I could feel the connection right away. I liked you. You must be related to me somehow, and don't know it."

"Oh, I know it. And I am related to you in more ways than you know, just as Lawrence is related to you as well, and not just because he is a distant cousin.

"But I have to explain. Your grandfather was keeping some secret from you. He had kept some secret from your mother as well, but I haven't found out what any of those secret were. Only I realized that your mother was very unhappy, because of that secret, and the fact that he would not reveal the truth to her until it was too late for her to have happiness with the man she loved. I had been keeping the truth from you as well. I wanted to save you from the pain and sorrow. Maybe your grandfather wanted to save your mother from some pain and sorrow as well, I don't know, but she hated him because of that truth he had kept from her, and she ended up taking her life because of it.

"I found the newspaper clipping and the suicide note she left. I will let you read them later, after all of this sinks in." She patted Amelia's hand, watching for some sign of shock, but Amelia just nodded.

"Please continue," she said. "I have known all along the things about my mother couldn't be good, since my grandfather wouldn't even mention her name, and locked that room with all of her things in it."

Loraine, took in her breath, and then forded on. "Your mother did not die giving birth to you, as I assumed. She killed herself because of some information her father had told her that he had been keeping from her all her life. She said in her note that she could not bear to have to tell you the truth, and hoped that her father would be brave enough to tell you himself. She said she hoped that by raising you, it would remind him that keeping the truth from her had ruined her life and made it into a hell, when she finally found out. That it would have been better not to hide the truth from those you love. I know she loved you, because your father was her lover, the cousin that came from New York, and then disappeared."

"How did you find all of these things out? Did you find her diary?"

"No, and I am not psychic, either, or at least not in the way you may think. It all started when I tried on Loraine's wedding dress that was still hanging in her closet. Your grandfather had put everything she owned in that room, so you would never find them."

Amelia was looking through the album as she listened to Loraine's story, shaking her head in disbelief. Loraine surged forward wanting to get it all over with.

"When I put the dress on, it seemed like I was transferred back in time. I was your mother, Loraine, getting ready to marry Mr. Billings, the banker. That is why I knew she hated the banker, because I had her thoughts, and I did not want to marry that man. I loathed him, or she loathed him. But I believe that I was your mother back then. That I have been reincarnated as myself, and that while I am not related to you otherwise, I came back here to make it up to you somehow, because I left you at birth, and you would never know the truth about yourself, or your mother, unless I came here and discovered the answers for you. I had always been drawn to this house, even as a child.

"Somehow you knew there was some connection between you and me, because you advertised for me to come, and somehow Lawrence knew it, because he came at the same time, and we were immediately drawn to each other. I believe that Lawrence was your mother's cousin in the past, and they were lovers and soul mates. They came back here, not only to make it up to you, but to get back together, because for some reason he left her, or something happened to him which kept him from marrying her, the way he planned.

"The bad news is that I knew he was my lover in the past, and I didn't tell him. When he found out that I knew it all along and wasn't telling him, he got angry, and didn't think I wanted anything to do with him. He thought I was playing him in some way, and he stormed out of here because of it. I realized then, that keeping the truth from others only hurts them, and so I decided that no matter how bad the truth was, I had to tell you, and discover all the answers, until it was all uncovered, and it could not hurt anyone any longer."

Amelia gave a weak smile. "At this time of my life, it doesn't really make that big a difference, except for knowing about my mother, which you are telling me about. And now I know why I liked that young man so much. It wasn't just because he was my only living relative, but because he had a deeper connection to me than that. I have had eighty years to sit and wonder about my mother, and why my grandfather hated her so much that he wouldn't mention her name. Perhaps her committing suicide was one reason he never spoke about her, because it would have caused a stigma on the family, but I can't believe that was the only reason."

"He seemed to hate his nephew for some reason too, and

would have been enraged if he discovered that Lawrence planned to marry his daughter, to keep her from marrying Mr. Billings. By marrying Mr. Billings, it would save the business, only I have my suspicions that Mr. Billings was somehow undermining that business in order to force your grandfather to make Loraine marry him.

"That is something else I am going to have to discover. It seems to be getting easier for me to go back in time. I don't always have to put on the dresses to do it now. That is how I was discovering the answers, by putting on Loraine's clothes, and it would bring the memories back to me. Then Lawrence and I found the Lawrence of the past's suitcase up in the attic, when we went to look for your box of things. That is why we are suspecting foul play, since he disappeared, and yet his clothes remained here. Lawrence, opened the case, and started trying on those clothes, and then he started to remember his past life too. That is how he discovered he was my lover of the past, and got so angry at me for not telling him about it, when he discovered I knew he had been that lover."

"Well, this is a little much for me to take in right now." Amelia sighed. "But one thing, I know… that young man had better come back here and make things right. I did not go to all this trouble to have you look up my past, only to lose the two people who mean the most to me in this life. If you were soul mates, and my parents of the past, then it is only right you get back together, and remain together. Perhaps, together in this old house. I never knew what I was going to do with it, when I died, but now I know it really belongs to the two of you."

Loraine stared. "You are not going to leave us the house!"

"Who else would I leave it to and all my money too, for that matter? I have no friends or relatives that I know of. I thought it was going to end up becoming property of the State, since I had no one to leave it to. I know Lawrence doesn't need the money, but if he does not come back here and propose to you, I will leave it all to you!"

Loraine sat staring at her. She looked tired, but her face had a more relaxed expression on it. "Are you all right?" Loraine asked softly.

"Yes, yes, I am fine. And I am very happy, because I can feel content knowing who my father was, and that my mother truly loved him. Whether he disappeared, or she killed herself is not important now. What is important is that they do not lose each other in the future the way they lost each other in their past."

"I am going to solve this mystery, Amelia, and when I do, I will call Lawrence. My cousin, Randy has his phone number, but I want to wait until I have all the answers first."

Amelia gave a sad smile. "Life seems so tragic sometimes, it knocks us for a loop, and tries to do us in, but we can rise above it, if we try. I have been a prisoner of this wheelchair the majority of my life, but I have never given up hope, and you came to me when there was no one else to help me. He will come back to you, Loraine. I feel it in my bones."

"I hope you are right. Oh how I hope you are right," Lorain murmured, kissing Amelia on the cheek.

Loraine left Amelia, and went back to the locked room. She sat on the bed, searching the room with her eyes, looking for her own answers. She didn't want to leave the room now. Before, it had frightened her, and she felt stifled there, feeling she had been locked in that room at one point in her past life, but now it was the only place that held any answers for her. She decided she would stay in that room, sleep in that room, wear Loraine's clothes of the past, until everything came back to her.

She went to the dresser and pulled out one of Loraine's nightgowns. The material felt soft and inviting. It smelled of lavender because there had been a sashay in the drawer, and even after all these years, the faint smell still clung to the clothes. She pulled the gown over her head, and lay back on the bed, and found herself falling asleep immediately.

Loraine was awoken by voices, they were urgent, and hushed, and yet she could hear them, arguing. Arguing about her! She got up from her bed, and went to the hall. The voices were coming from her parent's room. She was in the past again, and she tiptoed down the hall and stood at her parent's door listening.

"We should have told her a long time ago!" It was her mother's agitated voice, almost shrieking at her father.

"Don't worry. There is no need to tell her now either. She should never discover it. What good would it do?"

"I knew he was attracted to her, the moment I saw the way he was looking at her. This would have never happened if..."

"I said I would take care of it. I am going to talk to him. After he hears what I have to say, he will leave here. We will get Loraine safely married to Mr. Billings, and then there will be nothing either of them can do about it."

"But I can see she loves him," her mother's voice sounded sad.

"It is natural for her to be drawn to him, they are related."

"It's not just that..."

"Well this can't happen. We both know this can't happen. Once I talk to him, he will leave, and never show his face here again, I am certain of it."

"She hates Mr. Billings. You can't make her marry the man." Her mother's voice sounded sad.

"It is the only thing that will keep her from chasing after him. Once she is married and takes on her wifely duties she will have to forget about him."

"Well, you had better do something about it soon. The

maid said she heard them whispering about plans to get married before Loraine is forced to marry Mr. Billings."

"The little upstart, he is just like his father!" Mr. Landon growled under his breath.

"He, like his father, is determined to have what he wants, regardless of the situation. Nothing will stop him, unless you tell him, and maybe even that won't stop him."

"Of course it will! Think about it. He can't possibly consider marrying her, once he learns the truth."

"Yes, yes, you are right. I just hope they haven't already done something stupid..." she trailed off.

"If he's anything like my brother, he may have, that is why we have to put a stop to this before it is too late."

The voices were quieter now, talking softly, as though the concern had been resolved, and Loraine turned away from the door. Something horrible was about to happen to separate her and Lawrence. What kind of truth would make him leave her? She couldn't believe he would ever leave her. He loved her, he had shown it by sharing her body, and he wanted to marry her. He had to marry her. Her breath caught.

She wasn't going to tell him until after they married, unless it made a difference, but she feared she was carrying his child. He had to marry her now! She would never let Mr. Billings father Lawrence's child, never, never, never. If her father tried to scare him away in some way she would tell him. Then he would want Lawrence to marry her regardless of whatever nasty truth her father was going to use as a leverage to separate them.

She went back to her room, and crawled into bed. When she woke in the morning, Loraine felt a strange agitation, as though there was something important for her to do, and then she remembered her dream, but it wasn't a dream. It was yet another memory of her past.

CHAPTER FOURTEEN

Lawrence was driving down the freeway, breaking the speed limit, as he pushed his BMW to its limit, passing cars like they were standing still. He didn't even care if he got stopped and was given a speeding ticket. He could afford a ticket, more than he could afford this paralyzing pain that was seeping through his body.

He had been standing there in the attic, putting on the shirt, feeling a dizziness as he looked across the room to Loraine, and then he could hear the surf in his ears, feel the sand under his feet, feel Loraine in his arms. His hand was pushing up her leg, his lips were hungrily pulling at her mouth, his head was spinning as he felt her softness under his fingers, pushing through the opening of her pantalets, finding that warm inviting spot, causing her to cry out in ecstasy as he fondled her, pulling her soul to the surface, making her reel with waves of discovery of what being a woman was all about.

At the same time, he could see Loraine in the attic standing there, staring at him, and he knew she knew. She had known all along, and held him off, except, for that one night. That one wonderful night when she let down her walls and let him enter a place in her heart he thought he would never be able to penetrate.

But that one night was fleeting, and then she had pulled away again, refusing to let him in for some unknown reason. Why? He loved her so desperately, and after spending that one night with her, he knew she was the only woman he wanted in his life, and yet she had played him, and pretended not to know. He scowled, and pushed on the accelerator even harder, racing to a hundred miles an hour. The speed his heart was pounding at the time.

He heard a sound, it was like a gunshot, and then the car was spinning out of control. He realized at the same instant that he had blown a front tire. He fought to hold the car on the road as it careened one way and then the other. He knew better than to put on the break, and just tried to steer the vehicle to the shoulder, as he took his foot off the accelerator, and allowed the car to slow its pace, while the tires squealed, leaving black marks on the pavement, as a permanent history of the mishap. Suddenly the car hit a road reflector, and plowed through it, pushing the pliable post over, which slowed the car even more, and then another road reflector, which caused the little BMW to bounce over and smash into a speed limit sight, causing the air bag to deploy, and smash him in the face, as he was thrown forward.

His head was spinning. He was on the beach again. He was in a cave, and Loraine was there. She was crying. She was yelling at him, she was demanding. She told him something, something he did not want to hear, something that shocked him. He was telling her to go away, to go back and marry Mr. Billings, but why? He loved her. He did not want her to marry the man. He wanted her for his own, and yet he was pushing at her, pushing away from her like he had done in the attic, walking away. Walking down the beach, his heart in his throat, his mind going mad, his head feeling like it was going to explode, and she was screaming at him. Calling him, telling him it wasn't so, that her father was lying. Only he did not listen to her. He knew her father had not lied. It was the truth, a truth that meant he could never marry her. And he couldn't face life. He just wanted to die! Just wanted to die…

"Mister, are you all right?" The voice sounded far away. He tried to open his eyes. What had happened? Where was Loraine?

"We had a car phone, and called the police. The ambulance should be here any time now."

Lawrence shook his head. It was coming back to him. He had had a blowout, but he hadn't died. He was still here. He had this sinking feeling. He had wanted to die…no…that was someone else…someone in the past that wanted to die. He was in the here and now. He had to live. There was an important reason for living now. It…it was because of Loraine he wanted to live.

He was running away from her, just like he had done in the past. Why would he do that? Why did he leave her back then? Why had he left her now?

"I hear the sirens," the man was saying. "Don't get out of the car. Just wait until they come for you and check you out. You could be hurt and don't know it."

Lawrence tried to focus on the man that was speaking, but his mind seemed to be a blur. It was filled with Loraine's face, the way she had looked in the attic, crying into his shirt, and the way she had looked on the beach, her face stricken, as she screamed that it wasn't true. What wasn't true? He was trying to remember, but he couldn't. And it hurt his head too much to try. And then he could feel himself sinking away, sinking away from all the worry and the turmoil, letting the blackness take him to a peaceful place where he wouldn't have to think.

When he came to, he was in the ambulance, speeding away to some hospital, he was sure. They had put something over his face. It must be an oxygen mask, he thought. There was an I.V. connected to his arm and something was dripping from it, going into his veins.

He tried to pull the mask away, but a paramedic, sitting next to him, stopped him from doing it. "Just lie still," he said. "I don't think you are hurt very bad. Probably shock that made you pass out, but they will do some tests when we get you to the hospital. No broken bones that we can find, but they will give you X rays, just to make sure, nothing is cracked. Just relax. We will take care of you."

Lawrence closed his eyes. He had to get back. He had to get back. This was going to detain him! And then the car; he would have to get another car, and call the insurance company. What was Loraine thinking about him? She must hate him for just taking off like that. She had been crying and he wouldn't even listen to what she had to say. His stubborn pride had taken over. His temper had gotten the best of him. Even Randy's pleading to give it some time before he chucked it all, had not stopped him. He was such a fool! Such a God damn fool!

****

Loraine, felt a chill wash over her. She didn't know why, but deep inside it made her shiver. Something had happened to Lawrence. She knew. It was a deep inner awareness, and the thought frightened her. Her throat restricted, and the tightness made it hard for her to swallow. He had to be all right. It had been three days since he left, but she knew it would take the better part of a week to drive all the way to New York, if he drove straight through, and even longer, if he stopped along the way for any reason. There was no way she could call to check on him. She knew he had a car phone, but she didn't know the number, and Randy only had his home phone number in New York. She tried to push the dreaded feeling aside. He would come back. He would come back, she promised herself.

She tried to distract herself. She still hadn't found the diary. Maybe there wasn't any diary. Besides she knew most of the events anyway. There were still a few things that needed to be discovered. Why the business was failing, why Mr. Billings was so bent on marrying Loraine, and what the secret was that Loraine's father had kept hidden from her. If she could find those answers, everything else would fall into place, and maybe she could discover why Lawrence had just disappeared.

The only answer was to keep on putting Loraine's clothes on, until she could discover what had happened. She didn't know what dress to try, the photos in the album didn't seem to inspire her, and she felt like she was wasting valuable time. Finally she just closed her eyes, ran her hand across the dresses, stopped at one and pulled it out.

The dress was a ball gown. She hadn't even noticed it there before, she thought, but it was the most beautiful thing she had ever seen, and yet something about it repelled her.

She ignored the shiver that went through her, and threw caution to the wind, taking her clothes off, and putting the beautiful lavender gown over her head. Working the tinny buttons and sitting down on the bed, to keep herself from collapsing on the floor, as the dizziness washed over her. That familiar dizziness that told her she was moving back to the past.

She rose from the bed and put the diamonds around her neck. She didn't want to wear them, but Gaston had sent them, and her mother insisted. They seemed out of place, a terrible reminder what was in store for her, if Lawrence did not save her from this fate. It was the ball to officially announce her engagement and the date of her wedding, and nothing she could do to plead off, would move her father, or Mr. Billings. However, they would have to drag her kicking and screaming to the altar, she determined. And when the minister asked her if she took that old egotistical fool to be her husband, she would tell him no!

She pulled the long gloves on that reached to her elbows. The gown was off the shoulder with small puffed sleeves, and had a princess waist, falling gracefully to the floor, with no petticoats, which caused it to whisper against her legs as she walked. She felt naked in it, as it hugged against her hips, moving with the sway of her body, as though it was a part of her. The styles were changing, she realized, enhancing the shape of a woman, instead of hiding it.

Mr. Billings was going to take her to the hall, where the ball was to be held, and she cringed as she thought about riding in his carriage with him, but there was no way she could get out of it. Gaston met her in the entry, and watched as she came down the stairs towards him. He had never seen such a beautiful woman in all his life, and soon she would be his to hold and fondle, and be his wife, to obey his every whim, and he knew he had lots of whims that he was going to request of her. Her grace as she hesitantly floated down the stairs towards him, struck him hard in his lower region, as the movement of each delicate leg, pressed against the material of her gown, sending desire throughout his body, while he watched her.

Finally she stood before him, and he took her hand. He could feel her trembling beneath his touch, and he loved the thrill it gave him. He could tell she was afraid, but it only fed his sense of power over her, and he wanted her shy and hesitant, so he could groom her in the way he wished.

Gaston helped her up in the carriage, and as she lifted her skirt to step up, he licked his lips at the sight of her slim ankle, and then his eyes moved towards her well-shaped breasts, which the dress draped over in such an enticing way and complemented. He could barely contain himself. He had not brought a driver. He wanted her to himself, and since they were betrothed, he could get away with escorting her alone.

Loraine sat very still beside this man she detested. He was smiling and even his smile made her feel faint. They rounded a bend in the road, and he pulled the carriage off the main drive into the shelter of some trees. "Why have you stopped?" she asked as her voice cracked.

"To give you something," he told her, as he wrapped the reins around the break handle.

She was silent, and he pulled a long narrow box from his coat pocket.

"I wanted to give you something to complement the necklace," he whispered. He flipped the lid of the box and a beautiful diamond bracelet, which matched the necklace she was wearing, lay within the velvet lining.

"You have given me too much, already," she said. "I cannot accept it."

"Of course you can! I will soon be your husband, and you shall have all the bobbles that you want to adorn your body."

"I don't want bobbles. I don't want you. I will never marry you. I will not take any vows to honor, obey, or love you! Seriously, if you must know, I loathe you. You and my father can play this little game, if it pleases you, but I will not become your wife...NEVER!"

Gaston felt his temper rising, but managed to control it. "Don't be so ungrateful! I will be saving your father from ruin by marrying you."

"You are probably the reason for my father's pending ruin," she spat at him.

"How dare you say that, hasn't your father taught you any

manners? By God, when you become my wife, you shall learn better manners than that."

"I shall never become your wife, sir," Lorain spat, as she glared at him, in disgust.

He sat for a moment and stared at her. Then he brought his head very close to her ear. "If you don't want any trouble, young lady, you will not balk at becoming my wife. I am a very powerful man. If you think your father is having difficulties now, wait until I am through with him! If you defy me, he will end up in the poor house, mark my word." Then he smiled, and held out the bracelet. "Put it on and see how it looks," he said as though there had been no threat between them.

She blinked at him, partly in disbelief, and partly to hold back the tears that were pricking her lids. Like a sleepwalker, she held out her wrist for him to latch it over her glove, as he smiled at her with those diabolical eyes of his, staring down the front of her dress, while he placed the bracelet on her wrist.

"Now, show your appreciation by kissing me," he demanded, and not waiting for her to comply, he pulled her to him and put his mouth over hers, trying to thrust his tongue into her mouth, as he held her head tight against his assaulting lips, but she stubbornly kept it closed. She could hear him growl under his breath, but distracted himself by pushing his other hand under the neck of her gown, finding her softness and crushing it with his fingers.

Loraine struggled against his kiss and his hands, but he grabbed her wrist, and twisted her arm behind her back. "Come, my sweet, do not fight against the enviable. I am the man you will soon be sharing your bed with. No reason to be shy."

As he held her arm with one hand, he continued to take advantage of her, bruising her soft delicate skin, as he snatched at her, causing her to cry out in shock.

"You brute! Unhand me!" Loraine burst, struggling to be free of his mouth and the hand holding her wrist.

Gaston only chuckled, taking his hands and pushing both sleeves of her gown, even lower over her shoulders, to expose her pale body to the moonlight, smiling as she squirmed to be free of him.

"Now, now, we do not want to rip this beautiful dress, do we? It would be a shame. Then you could not attend the ball, and I would have to take you home with me, to make repairs on the dress. And while that was being done, well, I am sure we could find a way to entertain ourselves."

His words, stunned her, and stopped her struggles. He smiled triumphantly. "That is much better, my dear. I knew you would see it my way. Let me have a few thrills now, and we shall save the rest for later, when we are legally married. You are so, so beautiful. I can barely wait until our wedding night, I must take a few samples before that time arrives, I am afraid, but I am sure, you understand."

Loraine shook her head, but could say nothing. She knew nothing she said would affect this man, and now that he had her cooperation, he continued his onslaught. His mouth pulled at her skin, his hands searched out her curves, as he explored her body, keeping her mouth captured, while he played her with his hands, and then distracting himself, as his tongue slid over her skin, and licked at her like a starving wolf.

Because she was no longer struggling, he took even more liberties by shoving his hand beneath her skirt, searching for her. Loraine tried to back away from his touch, but when she did that, his mouth clamped down harder on her, as a warning of what he was capable of, if she proved to be difficult, and she was forced to accept his rough caress.

She sat stiffly in shock, as he made what Lawrence had done in love seem ugly and degrading, and painful, bruising her very soul in his mad desire to conquer her spirit. But that did not seem to be enough for him. He started to pull a glove from her hand, and at first she could not understand why he was doing it?

"You must touch me too," he whispered, his breath out of control.

Gaston unbuttoned his trousers, and placed her hand on him. "See how nice that feels? Here, yes, come now, don't be timid, if you do not comply I could satisfy myself with your body before our wedding night. It would be such a shame, but I am capable of it, do not fear." The sound of his voice caused trimmers to race through her, because she knew he would be true to his word, if she refused him.

Loraine gasped, and wondered if her touching him would even stay his hand or would he try to take her anyway, regardless of what she did at his command?

"I know you like this," he chuckled darkly. "You are just playing coy. Once we are married, I shall show you so many more things you can do to please me." He promised. "Now, don't stop. You are acting as though your arm does not have the ability to move, when I know it does."

Loraine's stomach started to turn. He was debasing her with his insistence that she touch him the way he demanded, and tears started to trickle down her face. However Gaston seemed oblivious to her anguish.

"Oh, yes, oh yes," he was saying, as he slammed his mouth over hers, and she jerked her hand away.

"What? Don't you love the power you have in a simple touch? You may not know this, but it is what will bring us endless pleasure, and once we are married, I shall introduce you to the ways of bringing children into our lives. I must warn you, I plan to shower my physical love on you, endlessly. The very smell of you excites me beyond belief," he informed her, with a leering smile upon his face.

Her hell had been planned for her, she thought, and she would rather die, than marry this man.

"Oh, but you were not fulfilled, were you?" he mumbled. "It isn't fair that your need should be neglected."

"I am fine, I am fine," she told him. We will be late to the ball." She was struggling to push his hand from beneath her skirt.

"Are you sure? I don't want you to believe I am heartless."

It was the very thing she believed, but she managed to smile. "You have already made my skin tingle and my heart to race," she told him truthfully, but it hadn't been out of pleasure.

He began straightening her clothes, lingering his fingers on her breasts as he adjusted them beneath her dress.

"I cannot believe, how lovely you feel," he chuckled when he finally pushed her skirt back down, and then kissed her full on the mouth. It was almost more than she could endure, but she would live through it, she kept telling herself. She would get through it, and then demand that Lawrence take her away before Gaston could ever do something like that, and possibly worse, to her again.

Loraine sat in silence, as he laughed and chatted with her, once he whipped up the horses again and pulled the carriage out onto the road once more. He was acting as though nothing had ever happened, and when they finally entered the hall, he explained that his horse threw a shoe, and it took them forever to find a blacksmith that would come out at that time of night to replace it.

She stood listlessly beside him, refusing to look at him, or talk to him. At the risk of being reprimanded by him later, she walked straight away from him, and out onto the patio, and relief flooded through her, when she saw Lawrence standing there.

Without thinking, she rushed into his arms. "Take me away from here!" she demanded. "Take me as far away from here as you can!"

One look at her, told him that she was in some sort of shock, and the trembling of her body, confirmed it. He led her out across the grounds, and took her to his own carriage, without a word, and they rode in silence, until he had reached the house.

"Come with me onto the beach and tell me what happened," he told her softly. "I can't help you, if I don't know."

"We have to leave. You have to take me away right now! It will not help if we wait until just before the wedding. The man has no honor! He will force me, Lawrence. He tried to force me tonight."

Lawrence turned angrily towards her and stared into her frightened eyes. "Did he touch you, Loraine? Be truthful with me."

"It was horrible, Lawrence. He threatened to ruin father, if

I didn't marry him, and then he wanted to give me a sample of what married life would be like with him. I struggled and tried to stop him, but he threatened to take me to his house and finish the job, if I did not comply with his demands."

"What kind of demands?" Lawrence growled between clenched teeth.

"Intimate demands, Lawrence. He touched me everywhere, and it wasn't all gentle touching. He made me touch him. I cannot face him again, Lawrence. You have to take me away!"

More than just anger surged through Lawrence's body. He wanted to kill the man! He felt like getting a gun and calling him out, only that was not done in these modern times, and he would be accused of murder. He pulled Loraine to him to ease the pain in his heart and ease the pain in her heart. He would have to take her away, before the brute could do any more damage, but how was he going to accomplish that?

"Listen, Loraine, I know that somehow Gaston is responsible for your father's business failure, and if I can prove it, then your father will call off the wedding. It should only take me a couple of days to discover what hand he had in it. Stay in your room, and plead that you are ill. Do not let Gaston visit you, and do not leave your room for any reason, until I can clear the way. If that doesn't work, I will come and get you, and take you away. We have a week before the wedding, and that should give me enough time."

"I don't care about the business. Just take me away!" she begged.

"If I take you away, before proving Gaston's hand in all of this, he will hunt us down to get revenge. Your father would drag you back and make us have our marriage annulled. We have to make him see the villain that Gaston really is. It is the only way."

"Father wants to stop me from seeing you. The maids overheard us talking, and I heard my parents arguing about it. He said he was going to tell you something that would make you go away for good, Lawrence. Don't listen to him. Promise me that you will not go away and leave me!"

"Never... I will never leave you, Loraine. You are my life, my love, the only thing I live for. Nothing your father could do or say could keep me away from you. Believe me, Loraine. I love you! I shall never leave you."

The words kept repeating in her head, as she took the ball gown off, and found herself sitting on the bed, shaking at the remembrance of what Gaston had done to her, and the words of Lawrence's promise, and she knew he did not keep his promise.

No wonder she hated and mistrusted men! Gaston abused her, and the one person she loved left her. How could she trust men after all that, even a man that she loved? After all, he not only left her in the past, but now he had left her in the future, as well.

****

The Hospital insisted on keeping Lawrence overnight for observation, just in case he had a mild concussion. They said he kept slipping in and out of consciousness, but he knew it was just his slipping in and out of time, trying to remember his past life. Trying to understand why he would leave his soul mate, the only woman he could ever love? Yet his head *was* splitting, and he didn't know if it was because of the accident, or because of his desire to discover the truth that refused to reveal itself. He was probably trying too hard. They gave him something for the pain, and it made him drift off again.

It was dark, and he was following someone. He had gone back to the engagement ball, so they would not think he had been with Loraine. He knew Gaston would be angry when she was not there at the time their engagement was announced. It would be humiliating, but he deserved to be humiliated, after what he had done to the girl. He should have realized that what he had done would scare her out of her wits, and she would try to escape any way she could. The man was insufferable, and his ego gave him a sense of power, which altered his common sense. He was so sure he could manipulate Loraine and her father into doing whatever he wished. Perhaps the father would fall into his trap, but Lawrence was sure Loraine never would. She would kill herself first, he was sure.

The thought brought him such deep pain, that his breath failed him, and he had to stop and lean against a lamp post, which turned out to be a good thing, because right at that moment, he saw Gaston pause, and then from the shadows of an alley two men appeared.

Lawrence crossed over to the same side of the street, keeping to the shadows himself, as he edged closer to the group, who were in quite discussion.

"I have another job for you," he was telling two rough looking men, who were not dressed in expensive clothes, which indicated they were not in Billings' realm of wealthy friends. These were rascals of the street, who could be hired to do anything from theft to murder, and Lawrence knew it was significant that Billings was meeting them, especially tonight.

He had seen the look on Billing's face, when he could not find Loraine at their engagement ball, questioning her parents about her whereabouts. Of course the man knew why she had fled. It had been his own fault, but still he looked like he was fit to kill someone over it. Of course, they couldn't just stop the ball, so it continued, and when the announcement of their engagement was made, the guests were informed that Loraine became ill and had to return home. Well that part was practically true. Billings had made her ill, and she did return home.

Lawrence knew Billings was angry, and wanted to make sure he did not appear back at Loraine's home, and cause some scene, so he followed him, but instead, he was lead to this back alley where Billings was planning something with these men. He couldn't get close enough to them to hear all that Billings was saying, but he could tell by the expression on Billing's face, proffered by the soft glow of the street lamp, that he wasn't just passing the time of day with the men.

They parted company, and Lawrence decided that instead of following Billings, because it was too late for him to return to the Landon's home and request a visit with Loraine, that he would follow the two thugs and see if he could gain any more information, concerning what kind of job Billings had required them to do.

His quest led him to the seedier side of town, and to a small shack, where the men entered. It was an abandoned home, that the street people usually used for shelter. Since the windows had long been broken out, it was not difficult for Lawrence to hear their conversation, once he stationed himself beneath one.

"I don't know, Dan, it was risky setting that place on fire like we did, and then grabbin' those shoes and getting rid of them, but I don't like the smell of this."

"Listen, Joe. We didn't get caught for the other lot. Billings will watch our backs."

"Unless it suits him to get rid of us, like he so easily wants us to get rid of other people. What's to keep from double crossing us, and doing us in as well?"

"He hasn't done anything to us so far," Dan pointed out. "Bring over that whisky, and let's have a taste of it. I am as dry as a bone." Lawrence heard one of the men shuffle across the room and then the clink of glasses, as one of the men placed them on a table, or some surface.

"You should be worrying about the safety of your bones, instead of complaining of how dry they are," the voice was gruff. "I don't like it. Starting fires and intercepting packages is one thing, but murder…"

"He didn't say anything about murder. He just said to get rid of the man, that don't mean killing him."

"How else would you get rid of a man?" The sound of liquid being poured into glasses filled the pause.

"We could hit him over the head and cart him off. Tie him up and put him on a boat, or train, or something, so as how when he finally woke up, he would be far away from here. It's only a week till the wedding. That's all the time Mr. Billings said he needed."

"But that wouldn't keep him from coming back, if you know what I mean."

"I'd be too late by then. The sweet thing would be married

to Billings by then."

"But how we gonna do it? We gotta get close to the man first."

"There are always opportunities, if you try hard enough to find them."

"If you keep drinking like that, you will be flat on your face, when the time comes."

"Don't worry about me, pal, I can hold my liqueur."

Lawrence remained, but they didn't say much more. They kept drinking, and pretty soon he heard one snoring, so he crept away.

Someone was to be done away with, so Billings could marry Loraine. He knew it wasn't Loraine's father. He was all for the wedding. That only left one man to be rid of... himself. Billings must know, like Loraine's father knew, that he would marry Loraine, before he ever allowed Billings to marry her. Well, he had the information he wanted. Now all he had to do was inform his uncle of it, and the wedding would be called off.

No man in his right mind would allow his daughter to marry someone who had tried to destroy their business. And after he described what Billings put Loraine through, there would be no way for him to approve of his daughter's marriage to such a fiend.

Lawrence could hear the nurses walking around his room, and he slowly opened his eyes. It was morning. He had been in this place all night. He had to get out of here, and get back to Loraine, and tell her what he had discovered about that past life. He was just as much a part of it, as she was, and that was why they had turned up at the same place at the same time. It was fate for them to find each other again, and this time, he had to make it right. He only hoped she would forgive him for taking off like that. She had to forgive him, he muttered under his breath.

CHAPTER FIFTEEN

Loraine sat staring at the wedding dress still hanging in the wardrobe. What had happened? Lawrence was supposed to take Loraine away before she ever could get married to Billings, and yet, the very first day she had gone back in time, she had put on the wedding dress, and plans were going forward for the wedding, so what had happened to Lawrence? Why hadn't he come and taken her away? Had he left, or had something happened to him? There was only one way to find out. She had to put on the Yellow dress, and go out the window to find Lawrence. That had been what she was about to do on that very first day. She had put it off. Held it at bay, because she was afraid to find out what had happened to Lawrence.

Now Lawrence was on his way back to New York, and the Lawrence of the past, had not come and married her like he had promised. Was history going to repeat itself? Would her life never be saved from the heartache of the past, and would it continue with heartache into the future? Why would God put her through this again? Or was she putting herself through it again? Maybe she had not learned anything from her past mistakes. If that was the case, she would have to go through it all again!

Loraine could not face the thought of living without Lawrence in this life in the same way she had to live without him in her last life.

Why else would they have come together, if not to find each other again, and find a way to change what happened to them in the past, and finally share the love that was deprived them back then? She swallowed hard, as she slowly walked to the wardrobe, and removed the yellow dress. She laid it out on the bed, and just looked down at it. Did she really want to find out? She knew it was not happy, because in the end, Loraine returned to the house, never to see Lawrence again. She had stayed in this room, had Lawrence's daughter, and then killed herself out of remorse. What truth was so horrible that it caused Loraine to take her own life back then? It was time to find out, she resolved.

With trembling fingers, Loraine lifted the dress, and smoothed her hand over the material. The very feel of it, frightened her. Slowly she removed her own clothes, and then with determination, before she changed her mind, she grabbed up the dress and pulled it over her head, did up the buttons, and sat on the bed.

She was at the window, looking back at her room, knowing she would probably never see this room again. What had happened to Lawrence? He was supposed to come and get her, and now the wedding was upon her, and he still had not come. He had told her that if he could not convince her father to call off the wedding, he would come and get her, and they would elope, and yet he had not come.

What if something had happened to him? She could not bear the thought. Surely her father would not do anything to him. He was his nephew, and he would have his brother to answer to if he did something to Lawrence. As far as she knew, Gaston did not know about her relationship with Lawrence, so he would have no reason to do anything to Lawrence. So either something happened to detain him or he had decided not to come.

Loraine could not believe that Lawrence would just not come. If he had changed his mind, he would have come and told her, but she had done what he had told her to do. She had stayed in her room, claiming she was ill, so her mother most likely would not allow Lawrence to see her. But he could have come at night. He had come to see her in her room at night before. She hadn't told him she was carrying his child. Now she wished she had. Then he wouldn't have let anything stop him from coming to her!

She climbed down the trellis, fearing that someone would catch her before she could get away from the house, but they were all out in front, waiting for her to come out to the carriage. She escaped out the back, across to the beach, and started following the shore. She would go to the cave. He would know where to find her. It was their secret rendezvous place. When she didn't show up at the church, he would know. Certainly, he had not left her.

He would stay to try and find a way to stop the wedding! Maybe he was planning to step up, when they asked if anyone knew any reason why the two should not wed, to speak up or forever hold their peace. She prayed he would come, so she waited.

She waited. She could hear people calling for her, wondering up the beach, but she waited. He would come, she told herself. He would come. And she waited.

The sun was starting to set, when a shadow appeared in the entrance of the cave, and he was there. She rushed to him, and threw herself at him.

"Where were?" she demanded. "You were supposed to come and take me away? I am so glad you are here! You don't know how much I worried that something horrible had happened to you!"

He stood stiffly. He was not holding her to him, like she thought he would. What was the matter? She pushed back from him, and looked into his face. His face was cold, and flat, and she could tell he had been crying.

"What is the matter, Lawrence? Tell me what the matter is!"

He seemed to ignore her plea. "Why are you here? They couldn't find you. I knew where you were, but I had to wait until they stopped searching the beach."

He wouldn't look into her eyes, and this frightened her. "I

came here to find you! You said you would come and get me, but you didn't come. Were you going to let me marry Gaston?" she demanded, starting to feel a surge of anger and fear mixed.

"I cannot stop it. I tried, believe me, I tried!" Lawrence hung his head in despair and resignation.

"But you said we would elope if you could not stop it," she insisted. "Why did you just give up? You promised, Lawrence!"

Lawrence merely stared at her, without saying anything at first. It was like he really didn't want to tell her why he had not come.

"I talked to your father," he said at last. "I told him about Billings. He was the one who had your father's factory burned down, and then had someone intercept the orders. He was angry, yes, he was angry, but he said it didn't matter now, because Billings would make everything right, if you married him. So then I told him how Billings had treated you on the night of your engagement Ball. He was angry. Yes, he was angry, but he said that since Billings had compromised you, it was just as well that you married him."

"But you had compromised me as well! I should marry you, not him!" Loraine insisted.

"You would think so," he said this very sadly and his voice broke.

"I won't marry him. I am carrying your child, so father

will have to let me marry you instead!"

Lawrence's head jerked up. "What?" His eyes were wide... almost frightened-looking.

"Yes it is true! You are going to be a father!" Loraine admitted, at last, hoping it would turn the tables back to their original plan. Instead of the joy, she expected to see on his face, there was horror instead.

"Oh, God...what have I done? What have I done?" he wailed, and stood staring at her, as he shook with sobs.

"Shhh, shhh," She held him to her, but he pushed her away.

"Remember that 'truth' your father said he was going to inform me of? That truth, that would make me leave and never come back?" he questioned, as he held her at arm's length. She nodded, tears starting to streak her face as well, as she saw the look on Lawrence's face. "He told me what it was, Loraine. Did you know that your mother and my mother are sisters?"

"No...I didn't know that," she admitted. "So what does that have to do with anything? It only means we are double cousins," she reasoned.

"Double cousins are practically like brothers and sisters," he whispered, "but it gets worse..."

"I...I don't understand." Now Loraine was starting to shake a little.

"We are brother and sister, Loraine! That is why I can't

marry you!" he gulped, at last.

"What! That is absurd!" she shrieked.

"It is true. My father married your mother's sister, and she came and lived with them because their parents were dead, and she had no other place to live. When my mother was carrying me, my father seduced your mother, and she ended up carrying you. She was frightened, and didn't know what to do, and confided in your father, who of course, is not your father. But he felt he should do the right thing, and protect her from the embarrassment of having a child out of wedlock, and the family scandal of his brother being the father. So he took her away to the other side of the states, and married her. My father never knew he was your father. No one ever told him.

"Your father merely told him that he knew about his abuse to your mother, and that he was taking her away so it would never happen again. And then he never spoke to his brother again, or would have anything to do with that side of the family, except for businesses purposes.

"That is why, your father was upset when he discovered you had fallen in love with me, and I with you. He could not allow us to marry. If he told me, then I would leave, and you would never learn the truth. He was right. I would have left, because I cannot marry you now!"

Loraine felt her heart plummeting to her toes. "It isn't true!

My father is lying! He would say anything to keep me from marrying you. He hates his brother, and he hates you! He has made this story up, in order to stop us from getting married!" she insisted, clinging to one last hope.

"Why would he make it up? That would put a terrible accusation upon your mother!" Lawrence pointed out.

"Maybe she wasn't with child at the time. Maybe she just wanted to get away from his brother, and maybe she was in love with him, and wanted him to marry her, so she told him she was carrying his brother's child."

"Do you believe your mother of such treachery?" Lawrence questioned.

"Then I don't care. I am carrying your child. We have to get married!"

"What kind of marriage could we have? Even if this child was healthy and had no inter-bread deformities, we could not risk having any other children. That would mean abstaining from being lovers. We could not risk it. What kind of life would that be, not being able to express our love for each other? It would never work. It would be like a living hell! And the law would not allow it anyway. I cannot marry you. You should have married Billings! Then he would have believed the child to be his."

"I would never let Billings raise our child!" she spat, "Never! Besides I detest the man! He is cruel and he tried to ruin my father! I would kill myself before I would marry him! I would rather raise our child on my own, a disgrace to society, than marry that man!"

"I have ruined you, Loraine! No one will ever marry you now! How can I face myself? You should hate me for putting you through this!"

"No...I could never hate you. I didn't know about our relationship, and neither did you. It was not our fault. I loved you. I still love you!"

"Go back, Loraine. Go back and marry Billings. At least then you will be respected, and he will think it is his child."

"Like I thought I was my father's child? Never, I will not deceive my child, like my father has deceived me!" she ranted, clinging to his hand, hoping to change his mind.

Lawrence turned, from her, pulling his hand free, and ran from the cave, down along the shoreline. She could hear the sobs that racked him. She called after him.

"Don't leave me, Lawrence! Don't leave me! My father was lying! He had to be lying!"

But the sound of her voice was swallowed up by the sound of the waves crashing against the shore, like the crashing in her own heart, and she felt like she was drowning, as waves crashed over her. Waves she could not stop from crashing down, and she sank to the ground, as sobs racked her as well. What was she going to do? What was she going to do? She didn't think she could live without Lawrence.

It was a long time, before she lifted herself up from the floor of the cave. It was dark outside, and she stumbled out on the beach. She would not go home. She would go to the church. The same church she was going to get married in and throw herself upon the mercy of the nuns, and insist they give her shelter. She would never go home!

But she did go home. A week later, her father retrieved her, and returned her to her room. Since she refused to marry Mr. Billings, she was locked there until the baby was to be born, and then, her father told her, he would remove the child and find a home for it. No one would know she had even had it. More secrets…more secrets to keep, and her child would not know who her parents were! She would not be able to raise it, like she planned, and so there would be nothing to live for. No other man would have her, and she didn't want any other man, anyway.

Loraine's head was filled with the thought of nothing to live for, once the baby was born. She tied the sash to the leg of the table, and pushed it up to the window. She put the other end around her neck. She climbed out onto the trellis…

Loraine woke with a gasp, as she put her hands to her throat, and pulled the dress off. Everything in the room was spinning around her. She thought she could hear the baby crying.

It was the last sound her other-self had heard as she repented for what she was about to do, but still stepped off the trellis to her death, hoping God would understand. Where had Lawrence gone, after he left her in the cave? Lorain, along with her past self didn't know. How would she ever find out now?

****

Dealing with the insurance company was a nightmare! Lawrence had to discover where they impounded his car, and then the insurance adjuster had to make an appointment to appraise the car, and that took up two more days. Two more days that he had to remain where he was. Once they had decided the car was totaled, he had to wait for the check to be issued, but that did not stop him from getting a new vehicle. He had plenty of money for that. He just gave them his bank account number, and where to deposit the check. But until all the paper work was signed, he was stuck there. And there was the police report as well, and they had to get the tests from the hospital to make sure he was not driving drunk when the accident happened. And he did get that speeding ticket, since they estimated his speed well over the speed limit of the freeway.

Finally, after three days, of being stuck, either in the hospital, or doing paper work, Lawrence was finally able to drive away in his new Trans AM, a little heavier car than his little BMW was, and a lot more powerful. It ate up the road as fast, but this time he decided he would stay within the speed limit.

He wanted to drive straight through, but he knew that would be risking another accident, and he wanted to be sure to get back all in one piece, and beg Loraine to forgive him for high tailing it out of there like that, without letting her explain.

Lawrence drove as long as he could before he finally pulled over to a motel. He didn't even care what it looked like. He just wanted to crawl into bed and sleep, so he could continue his trip as soon as he could. He fell asleep as soon as his head hit the pillow.

The sound of the surf was pounding in his ears. He was running on the shore, running as fast as he could. He was trying to get away, and then he realized that he was trying to get away from himself. He couldn't run fast enough to get away from himself. And her screams were echoing in his ears. She was begging him to marry her anyway. How could he? How could he face his own father again, after what he had done to Loraine's mother? How could he face his life again? There was nothing for him. She was having his child and he would never see it, and he could never marry her.

He just wanted to die, he just wanted to die! Yes. That was the only answer. There was nothing to live for anyway. He turned his course, and started running out into the surf. He could feel the water washing over him, washing away all his worries and cares. *Loraine, please forgive me for what I am about to do*, he was thinking. He felt the waves lift him up, and he let them take him, far, far out. Out so far he would never be able to swim back.

Lawrence woke in a cold sweat. He was gasping for breath. It felt like his lungs were filled with salt water, and he couldn't breathe. Everything had been so calm, so peaceful, as he watched himself sinking to the bottom of the ocean, and then he came washing up, out of the dream, and he knew what had happened to Lawrence of the past.

Yes, he had left her. He had left her permanently, the same way she had left her child. He had left her and her child, and he had to make it up to her. He had to come back to her. This time they would make it work. They were no longer related to each other. Even if they were, he didn't care. All he could think of was spending the rest of his life with Loraine. And then he thought of the child. Amelia was the child! Loraine was not the only one who came back to make things right for Amelia. He had returned as well.

He drug himself out of the bed. Left the motel room, and climbed into his car, and headed back out on the road, in the direction of La Jolla, where Loraine was, where his life was, where the future was, if he could just make Loraine see how much he loved her. How much he had always loved her, and how she could not hold her walls up to him any longer. They were soul mates, and he would have to make her see that, if it was the last thing he did.

CHAPTER SIXTEEN

Amelia was working on the doll house, putting the details into the pink room. She seemed contented, but Loraine knew there was one more thing she was going to have to tell her. Why Loraine had committed suicide, and why Lawrence had left her. It was not going to be easy, but she vowed there would be no more secrets. She would wash all the old pain away with the truth, and they would have to get through it together.

It was hard to think of Amelia as her daughter. After all the woman was old enough to be her grandmother, but she could not help but think of her as a lost child, as she worked on the doll house her grandfather...her cruel grandfather...had made for her. He was the one who caused the death of his daughter by threatening to take the child away, and continue to live a lie and pretend like none of it ever happened. And even then, he would not tell his granddaughter the truth either. What a horrible man he was, she thought. But he too had his demons, she supposed. Perhaps he deserved forgiveness, so she could stop hating him, even though she had never met him in this life.

Maybe that is what it was all about... forgiveness... forgiving Lawrence for leaving her, and forgiving her father for deceiving her, and forgiving herself for leaving her own daughter to fend for herself without a mother's love. They were all guilty of something, even her mother, who passed her off as her husband's child, and Lawrence's father for seducing his wife's sister. It was sad. They were all guilty of something.

Now she watched as Amelia labored over her life time project, almost completed in the same way Amelia's life was almost completed. This house and everything in it, was all that Amelia had ever known. It must have been sad to be a prisoner of her house and her wheelchair. Nothing could change the past, but Loraine vowed she would try to change the future. She only hoped that Lawrence would return. She had tried calling his home phone in New York, but no one answered, and she got tired of leaving him messages. Where was he? He should have gotten there by now.

With determination to do what was right, Loraine sat down beside Amelia, and patted her hand.

"I think I know most of the answers now," she said softly. "I know why your mother, or myself in that life, killed herself."

Amelia looked up from what she was doing, and gave a child-like smile. "Don't worry," she said cheerfully. "I at least will know the answers, and certainly there was no blame on me, because I was just an infant at the time."

"Yes, all or most of the blame should land on your

grandfather's head, but it was not just him. He was caught up in it all, the same as the rest of us, and just did whatever he could to preserve his own sanity. Perhaps the blame should be laid on his brother's head, who started it all, and who lost his son in the end because of his thoughtless actions."

"I am listening," Amelia said, wanting to hear the story from the beginning.

"Your grandfather's brother forced himself on his wife's sister, your grandmother, while his own wife was pregnant with Lawrence. She became pregnant with your mother, and yur so-called grandfather, married the sister, to protect her from having a child out of wedlock, and to keep his brother from the scandal it would have caused. He left to California, and led everyone to believe that Loraine was his daughter, when in truth she was his brother's daughter.

"When Lawrence showed up, and fell in love with Loraine, he was determined to marry her before her father could force her to marry Gaston Billings, but your grandfather got wind of it, and knew he had to put a stop to it, and the only way to do that was to tell Lawrence the truth, that Loraine was his half-sister, and he could not marry her. Not only was she his half-sister, but their mothers were sisters, which made the relationship even closer by blood. The only problem was, that Loraine was already pregnant with Lawrence's child...you...so it was too late to stop them from having children together. Only he still could not marry her, because it was against the law for sisters and brothers to marry, and so he was forced to leave her. She never saw him again. No one knows what happened to him.

"Loraine went to the church, because she refused to go back and marry Gaston, but eventually her father discovered where she was, and brought her back. When she refused to marry Mr. Billings, her father locked her in her room until the baby was to be born, and then he planned on taking the baby away and finding a home for it, so no one would know she ever had it. This is what caused Loraine to take her life. She had lost the only person she could love, and her father would make sure she could never even love the child that Lawrence had fathered. She felt her life was not worth living, if she could have either to love.

"I suppose when your grandfather found her dead, there was no stopping the scandal, and it would all come out in the wash, so he kept the child, his only true heir, since his wife was her grandmother, and his brother was her grandfather. So he didn't find a home for you. He kept you here, to continue to make your life miserable, in the same way he had made his daughter's life miserable, by keeping the truth from you as well, and never letting you learn anything about your mother, or your father, because he knew who they both were, and he knew his hand in the whole affair had caused her to take her life. And yet he could still not admit it to himself or anyone else."

Amelia nodded absently, as though none of it mattered any longer. "At least I now have you. I only wish Lawrence would return, then…"

She was interrupted by Mary opening the door to the parlor. "You have a visitor, ma'am," she informed Amelia. They both turned, and saw Lawrence entering the room.

Loraine jumped to her feet and merely stared.

"We overheard you at the door," Lawrence said in a low voice. "I see you know the whole story, except for one thing. What happened to Lawrence."

"You know what happened to him?" Loraine asked, her heart racing. All she wanted to do was rush into his arms, but her feet remained glued to the floor, where she had stood up in front of her chair when Lawrence entered the room.

"He was a coward." Lawrence almost hissed. "He couldn't face his life without Loraine. He couldn't face his father who had caused the disaster. He walked out into the ocean and drowned himself, leaving Loraine to shoulder the burden herself. And she was not strong either. Her father was too much for her, it seems, and so she gave up, just like Lawrence gave up, and Amelia was forced to continue to carry the burden for 80 years, the burden that her parents and her grandparents left her."

"But I forgive them," Amelia said, her voice barely audible.

"I just wanted to know. That is all. I even forgave my grandfather for pushing me down the stairs. I know he didn't mean it. I know my mother loved me. It was because she couldn't bear to live without giving her love to me, that she took her life. And she wanted to punish her father, for what he had done to her and to Lawrence by waiting so long before telling them the truth. But it can be fixed now. You two have a second chance to make up for all that sorrow. I knew you would come back, Lawrence. I told Loraine you would. True love always wins out in the end, doesn't it?"

Lawrence turned his eyes to Loraine, and the electricity that passed between the two pair of eyes, emerald against obsidian, filled the room. With calculated steps he walked to her, praying that she would not put that wall up between them again.

"I will never leave you again, Loraine, if you will only forgive me for my stupid act of running away. I should have stayed and faced it, but perhaps a little of the old Lawrence remained with me, and it was just easier to walk away than to fight for what I really wanted."

"It was my fault. I kept pushing you away. I wouldn't let myself love, because I feared getting hurt, like I had in the past…in my past life, that is. I knew the moment you walked away that I had always loved you, but I just couldn't admit it to myself, not until I saw you in Lawrence's shirt, when you were standing in the attic. But by that time, it was too late. You had *always* been the one, back in my past life, and in this life too. I was just too frightened to accept it."

"Accept it now, Loraine." Lawrence said in a chocked voice. "Accept me now!" He held his arms out, and she fell into them. "We were meant to be one, Loraine. We were always meant to be one, but we threw away our chance in that past. I am not going to make the same mistake twice. It has taken two lives, and no telling how many more before this, to make me come to my senses."

Loraine lifted her head, and looked into those penetrating eyes, that had always seemed to be able to look right through her and read her mind, and she knew she was where she had always belonged... in Lawrence's arms. She vowed to never leave them, but before she could complete the thought, she felt Lawrence's mouth covering hers, and the sound of Amelia's hands clapping, as her arms came up around his neck, and she returned the kiss. The kiss that spanned two lifetimes, and she hoped would span many future lifetimes as well.

THE END

If you liked this book please write a review.

Printed in Great Britain
by Amazon

64716574R00169